SLOPPY

By Jasmine Farrell

Acknowledgements

Whew!
This book was a journey.
A beautiful one though.
My completion of this novel could not have been
accomplished without experiencing life, patience, my
crew of beta-readers and editors.

For their continued support and encouragement:
Dominique Ramsey, Zhane'l, L. M. Reynolds and
Jasmine Henderson.

Thanks to my father, for always supporting my love
of writing and reminding me to hang in there. Your
love, patience and wisdom has always kept me. The
countless times you had my back will not be
forgotten.

To my caring, loving, and supportive partner Reign
Taylor: my deepest gratitude. Your encouragement
when the times got rough are much appreciated and
duly noted. I love you!

Table of contents

When I saw Tori's beads at the ends of her braids sway back and forth to Biggie Smalls', "One More Chance," I knew I wanted to share my Play-Doh with her. Her deep brown skin shimmered as she smiled. Her grin, devoured by her deep dimples, made my fingers feel jittery as she cackled at my multi-colored LEGO house. I remembered switching my head to the right and eyed my overnight bag.

"What?" Tori grinned.

"I got you something, Tori," I replied.

"What is it?"

She pounced up. Eyes wide and her beads jiggling as she swayed in anticipation.

I crawled over to my bag and rummaged for my two jars of Play-Doh. I pulled out both jars and held them in the air.

"Hey, can I have some, Roxy?"

"Of course. That's why I took it out. It's for you. Here."

I bent over, pushed a jar towards her direction and watched her squeal. She knelt, placed both arms in front of our LEGO houses, and slid them back. With one quick swoop, she grabbed the jar once it reached her rainbow socks. I watched as her toes wiggled flamboyantly. I crawled to her side and opened my jar as well.

"Let's make stars, Tori."

She closed the Play-Doh and gently placed it on the beige carpet. She wrapped one arm around me and pressed her lips against my cheek and held them there for a while. I'm pretty sure that my heart leaped to the top of my mouth.

"Thanks, Roxy. Yeah, let's make stars."

"Yeah, 'cause you're a star, Tori."

Her mother swung Tori's bedroom door open. "Ya'll are both 8-year-old girls, not stars. Jesus is the star. He's the risen King and our everything. Now come in this here bathroom and wash ya'll hands. Ya'll been playing in here with this door closed, ya'll ain't hear me callin' ya'll. I dun' called ya'll five times. Dinner is ready. Hurry up and wash ya'll hands so we can all say Grace. Everybody is downstairs."

We shuffled past her and skipped down the hallway to the bathroom.

As our hands wrestled each other in the water, our giggles alarmed Tori's Mama.

"Stop all that playin' 'round and get down here," she hollered from the bottom of the stairs.

We both looked at each other in the mirror and snickered. Tori had the same kinky coils as mine. Our parents refused to allow us to relax our hair.

I rubbed my hands together and watched the bubbles overtake my little fingers. I felt sprinkles of water hit my face. I looked at the back of Tori's head as she buried her hands into the brown hand towel that was on a wooden rack. I quickly flicked a soapy hand in her direction, and she flinched. I rinsed off and waited for her to step aside so I could dry my hands too.

"Oh yeah," she said as she spun around to face me. She pressed her lips to my right cheek. It felt as though a fluffy teddy bear patted my cheek. She skipped out the bathroom, and her footsteps rumbled down the stairs.

I was frozen until Tori's mother exclaimed, "Little girl, don't have us eatin' cold food. Get your butt down here!"

I hurriedly dried my hands as my smile remained plastered on my face for the rest of the evening.

The following morning, when my Mama was on her way to pick me up, Tori and I waited in the living room. As we watched cartoons on the couch, I finally returned the kiss back. I remember the dent my lips felt upon reaching her cheek. I liked her dimples.

A week later, Sunday morning, Mama was preaching about the right kind of love that men and women of God should pursue. We were members of Holy Ghost Saints of Mt Ararat for All Nations in East New York, Brooklyn. I felt up and down the soft, fuzzy fabric until one of the deacons, sitting next to me, grabbed one of my hands with a tight grip. I squealed. I looked up at him and pressed my lips tightly together, hoping he'd let me go. He nodded, tilted my chin up, and raised my pressed lips. He gave me a you-*better-not act-up- in-the-House-of-God* face in return.

He whispered, "Listen to your mother preach and stop the fidgeting with your clothes before you mess them up. She paid good money for that skirt. Act like a god-fearing young lady."

I looked down and felt my skirt again. I jolted my head back up and looked to my left to see Tori's smile. Her eyes were looking at my own and I knew what was next. As she slid off the pew and dug into her mother's church bag on the ground, I went into my little purse. I looked up at Deacon Brown and smiled at his fixation on my mother.

Eyes still on his gray beard, with every breath I slid my jar of Play-Doh out until it sat on the pew with me. One leg crossed over the other, I shifted my body slightly towards the left towards Tori's direction. I coughed twice as I opened the small jar of mushy goodness. Tori did the same as she yawned her Play-Doh jar open. She shaped hers into a purple heart. I nodded and shaped mine into a blue diamond. I lifted it up a few inches and raised my chin to her. She raised her purple heart and paused, then slid back to the floor and into her mother's bag to grab a pen. She scribbled on the Play-Doh heart and looked up at me.

Her mother yanked her right leg towards her hip and muttered into her ear. Tori's head lowered as she cupped the heart in her hand. Her mother pinched her thigh and retrieved the pen. Her mother looked at me and pierced my chest open with her eyes. Her hand levitated and motioned attention to watch my mother. I looked forward.

My mother was a regal woman, faithfully has the fragrance of Perry Ellis 360 lingering way after she leaves. The clicking of her heels sounds like elegance with a hint of fierceness lingering on the bottom of her shoes. She smiles when talking about Jesus and how proud she is of me when I do anything related to God. With one look, she can pin me down and close up my throat. She's the authority even when she's absent. Her voice booms even when she's calm, and she cooks as though her parents discovered spices. Beverley, my mother, was the first woman to become ordained in our church. My Mama is fierce. My Mama is strong. My Mama terrifies me.

"Don't let that Devil tell you that you need to look elsewhere!"

My eyes followed my Mama's hand as she snatched the Bible from the podium stand and raised it in the air.

"Everything you need is right here in this book; you ain't got to look no further. That includes love."

She placed the book down and walked away from the podium. She scanned the congregation and took a deep breath.

"How to love and who to love. That's right: who. Some people sittin' in these pews right now got a boyfriend at home, and they a man themselves. Some women sittin' up in these pews have lady lovers at home."

She went down the two carpeted steps from the podium and walked forward.

"I'm here to tell you that even though God is love, homosexual relations ain't love. The sun needs the moon and man needs woman. You can love your neighbor as you love yourself, volunteer at the soup kitchen and talk to God every day. But if you out here lusting the same sex, the altar is where is you have to be because that is not of God. But that's alright, because our God is a deliverer. Our God is a healer."

The entire congregation stood on their feet and clapped. A few shouted "Hallelujah!" while my head sank and my body slumped into the pew. "You better preach it this morning, Minister Patton!" Deacon Brown shouted.

Mama marched back up the two steps and returned behind the podium. She scooped up her reading glasses and pushed them onto her face. Mama's owl eyes gazed down at the Bible as she flipped through the pages before continuing, "Let us turn to 1 Corinthians 6:9-10, and then I want you place a pen at 1Timothy 1:9-10..."

I knew my Mama saw me and Tori just now with our Play-Doh. I mouthed the scriptures to myself as she read them to the congregation. I'd written them down ten times on a notepad for punishment after I told her that I wanted to marry a pretty girl and have lots of babies. Tori was forbidden to spend the night at my house after Mama caught us holding hands a little longer than we should have been.

"Saints, I want you know that it's just a sin like everything else. Greed, lust, lying, whoremongering and homosexual relations, all sin. Ain't none bigger than the other. Yes, saints, it does matter who you love."

She turned her head and squinted her eyes towards me.

"An abominable act is an abominable act no matter how nice, kind, and sweet you are. But there is deliverance."

After the church service ended, Tori made a mad dash to me and put my heart in her bag.

"Here," she said as she smiled.

I showed her my creation and said, "Look. I made it cause you're a diamond. You can keep it."

She wrapped her arms around me and giggled.

∞

When Mama and I arrived home later that evening, she looked at me for a while and began to pace. She muttered to herself and prayed for Jesus to deliver me from my immoral passions fervently. Her eyebrows were high and sweat glistened on her forehead. Her heels clicked to a beat that I began to hum to until she clapped her hands.

"What are you humming? I told you about that secular music in my house, Roxanne. I don't even want you to hum it, do you understand?"

"But Mama, I wasn't I was--"

My face swung to the right, and it felt as though bits of sand were rubbed across my face. I grabbed my cheek as hot tears began to fall.

"Don't lie to me, little girl. It's bad enough Deacon Brown told me that you were talking to Tori during service and had the audacity to take out that silly putty with her as if you were having playtime in school. The House of God is not playtime. Yes, you can have fun with Jesus, but that wasn't the time-- and stop all that crying before I give you something to cry about."

"Mama I was just trying to make something for Tori," I replied as I swiped the tears from my face.

"I know. I saw you. Tori ain't your friend, Roxanne. She is a temptation. You too young to understand, but know that how you feel about that girl is wrong. You know it's wrong. I showed it to you in the Bible many times. Stop this madness."

She placed her thumb on my cheek and her index finger under my chin. She pushed my face to the right to see the pink hand print she put on my face.

"Get outta my face and go wash your own with some cold water. Stay in your room until dinner is ready."

I did as I was told. As I was drying my face, I heard her talking to herself in the living room, "Nine years old and wound up in this mess. The devil is a liar and deceiver and he will not have my child."

I walked to her bedroom quietly and opened the door. I sat on the bed and let the noise of the radio fill the room. I eventually took out the heart Tori gave me and noticed the carving she made.

T+R=4ever.

Swallowed Bruises

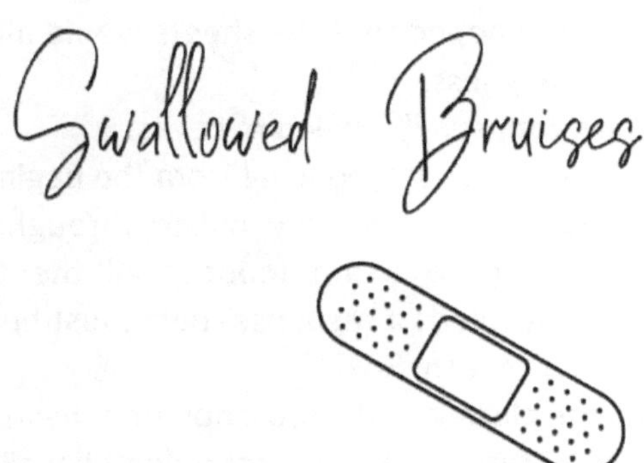

I always hated the lack of heat in Mama's apartment building. It was always cold in the living room where I slept. I love Brooklyn. I was born and raised in the Bed-Stuy neighborhood and this apartment is all I've ever known. Looking back, I was humming a song I made a few weeks ago about being trapped when my ribs made me wince in pain. I crawled back to bed and listened to the conversations that echoed from outside.

Two weeks prior to our first big break-up, Johnson wanted to marry me. When his name flashed on my phone that was on top of the pillow, I felt rage rise within me. He was probably calling to argue about some random thought he had in his mind about something I said.

I picked up the phone and gave him an introductory silence. Bypassing my notion, he asked how I was doing.

Without my reply, his tongue slithered, "I want to marry you, Roxy."

Two ice packs rested on my rib cage. A swollen thigh to compliment my blue pajama shorts, my heart felt heavy and once again, I ignored my intuition.

My body felt as though it were sinking into my twin-sized bed, and I hoped that the sheets would allow me to sink into nothingness.

"Really, Johnson?" I rolled my eyes.

"Yeah, girl. You stayed loyal from the beginning. This last fight was intense, but we pulled through. You just gotta stop being so damn mouthy all the time. Not everything I say needs a response, Baby. Just hear me out and close your mouth, Roxy."

"I'm not closing shit. You shouldn't have put your hands on me. Matter of fact, you shouldn't have lashed out in the first place just because I didn't want to meet up with you."

"Well listen, I apologized, and we're past that now. I won't do it again, I promise. I want you to be my future wife. I can't be treating my wife any kind of way."

I looked up at my white ceiling and observed the little cracks in various places. I anticipated the day it would all come crumbling down on me. If I was dead, then at least there would be no way for Johnson to reach me.

I knew I needed to leave Johnson, but the world already saw us as the perfect couple. Our faces, as a unit, were already plastered all over social media, and I couldn't bear the responses I would get if I left him.

"There you go again." He chuckled. "So, what's up? You down to be my Queen?"

The idea of marriage was sweet to my ears yet sour to my gut.

"Yeah, but I don't want an outlandish ring. Something small will do," I replied.

He grunted.

"Ring? You don't need a ring. My love is enough, Baby. Besides, we can use that money for more important things."

I shot up and my body slammed right back down. My entire being ached, and I wanted to throw the pain at him.

"I want a ring."

"We can get that after we're married, Roxy."

After the last argument, I didn't have energy left to argue.

"Fine."

"Great. My mother mentioned how we were together for so long and she asked why I didn't marry you yet. I didn't have a response. I realized that you're the one for me, Roxy."

My chest felt as though it was vibrating like a massage chair. If his mother didn't ask that question, I'm sure he wouldn't be asking for my hand in marriage. Vanity first for Johnson. I knew he was serious about marrying me. Being married to him would make him look good to his parents, I'm sure. With the last argument swirling in my mind and that ho-hum proposal, I was overwhelmed.

"I gotta go, Johnson. I need to rest some more."

"Okay, bye for now," Johnson replied.

I breathed normally once I hung up the phone. Thankfully, it was Saturday, and I had two more days until I had to return to work. I struggled to the bathroom and looked at my reflection.

I'm going to marry Johnson.

My stomach twisted.

I remembered when he uttered lines that were below the belt. Flashbacks of the consistent arguments and countless times I allowed him to overstep my boundaries bombarded my mind.

"That's your problem, Roxy. You won't let a man be a man 'cause you too busy saying no all the time."

My reflection was drowned by my tears, but I fought myself to keep them from leaking from my eyes.

My ex-girlfriend's face flashed in my mind. Karla's thin lips, painted gold with lipstick shimmering, smiling gently moments before she laughed. The eloquence of the red dress that complimented her shape the last time I saw her, made my heart dizzy.

I shook my head and rushed out of the bathroom. I snatched my laptop from the couch and plopped back on my bed. I looked up various divorce lawyers and the definition of annulment. I glossed over the various links and shivered at the plethora of information.

I clutched my jawline tight, hoping that if I clenched tight enough, I would shatter like glass. I just wanted to be swept up, thrown away and never to be seen again. I *had* to marry Johnson. He already met my mother and friends. My mother liked that his parents led a church and that he was a Christian. Well, at least he tells people that he's a Christian.

I shook my head and returned my focus to my laptop screen. I read what I typed into the search engine and felt heavy.

"I can't do this."

The heaviness lifted, and I called Johnson to decline the proposal. As the phone rang, I tapped my laptop keys. I wished on everything I could that he wouldn't pick up.

"What?" he sang into the phone.

"Listen, I don't wanna' get married right now. It's too soon. I'm not ready. We don't even have a plan. I want a ring and—"

"—Ah," he interrupted, "so this is what this is about! You want a ring. Roxy, listen, don't let society tell you what you want. You don't want a ring. You have my love and affection. That's all you need."

"This isn't about society. I want a ring. Me. I also said that I wasn't ready and this is too soon for me."

"Roxy, we've been together for seven months, and my mother encouraged us to just get married already. We've already been through enough together. We always come back to each other. So, why not just get married now? You not going anywhere and I ain't either."

"No. I am not ready, Johnson. I'm sorry."

I heard nothing.

I looked at my phone screen and read *call ended.*

I threw my phone back on the bed and walked over to my three bins that sat adjacent to the entertainment set. I lived in a one-bedroom apartment with my Mama. It was smaller than cozy, but I was thankful that I had a place to stay. I ripped off the top bin and snagged the first shirt I saw. I grabbed a pair of jeans and dug around for socks. I had an armoire in my mother's bedroom that held my intimate apparel and the rest of my clothes. Despite the bruises and aches that slowed me down, I had to get out of the house. I got into the shower to let the water wash away some dry blood and anxiety from my shoulders.

I remembered how I used to be a year ago. I was rooted in myself. Before him, I was dating Cynthia who had the lightest laugh. She could have torn my heart to pieces, and I would've created a whole album just to win her back. I let her go once things started getting too serious. Mama doesn't know I like women—or I least I don't think she does. Ever since my little girl-crush when I was nine, she never heard me utter to her about another woman since. Cynthia had kept asking me to meet my Mama and go on vacations, but I needed a roof over my head. So, I had to let her go. I stopped singing once Johnson and I were four months into dating. I reminisced the last time I really sung from my heart as I rubbed the soap maliciously against my washcloth.

∞

I remember squinting my eyes due to the spotlight. I barely saw the three judges that sat near a table about six feet away from the stage. I closed my eyes and sang an original song about secretly sleeping with a co-worker. I sang it acapella and swayed to the music in my head. I heard them snap along to my song and then suddenly they stopped. I heard a door slam loudly.

Johnson was in the back of the room glaring at me. With his guitar in tow, ready to strum, he waited for the judges to say something. I spoke up first.

"Oh my. I am so sorry. This is my boyfriend, Johnson. What a surprise."

One of the judges smiled and ignored my statement. She turned to Johnson and said, "Young man, I know you would like to be supportive, however this a private audition. You must wait outside."

He replied, "But I was allowed to be in here for the first audition."

"Yes, but this is the finalist round. Usually, your girlfriend would be disqualified for your outburst, but we'll let it go this time. Please leave so we can continue reviewing your girlfriend's lovely piece."

Johnson stomped his foot and yelled, "But I taught her everything she knows. I can play the guitar for her while she sings. I can also sing, you know. I can also play several instruments and..."

I balled up my fists. "You didn't teach me. How dare you make this about you. Judges, I assure you, this is my original song and everything about my vocal abilities is true in my bio."

Startled by my response, the judges asked for me to leave along with my boyfriend.

Johnson smiled at me and placed one of his hands out for me to hold as I walked towards the door.

"You wouldn't have been told to leave if you would've just shut up and let me play for you," he whispered.

I walked past his hand and out the door. I rushed out of the hallway and out of the Dynasty Theatre.

He skipped behind me and said, "Wait up. Why didn't you go along with this? If you would've just followed my lead and stopped being the boss all the time, then you could've nailed that audition!"

"It was my audition, Johnson. Not yours. Mine. You had no right to intrude."

"I was only trying to be there for you," he shot back.

I realized at that moment, we were yelling in the street, and people gave us stares. I walked away.

"I don't need this shit. Oh, and happy birthday, Roxy," Johnson screamed.

∞

I let the water rinse off the soap and exhaled slowly. I haven't sung since that embarrassing audition. Maybe I should've introduced the judges to Johnson and let him play.

Why I didn't let him go that day will be an eternal mystery.

After I moisturized my skin, I finally looked at my phone for any text messages. I had one from Johnson that read:

I need radio silence from you today.

Naked and appalled, I called him up and we proceeded to argue. When I hung up on him, I looked down at my bruises. I heard my mother's heavy footsteps.

I quickly wrapped my towel around me to cover the bruises. Once I heard the bathroom slam shut, I called him back and told him to never put his hands on me again just because he can't have his way.

He replied, "I forgive you," and hung up.

Patricia And Last Resorts

The following week after, Johnson sent a text saying he was outside my workplace. I walked over to the nearest window from my desk and saw he was standing under a tree.

Six feet and four inches tall, his relaxed 4c hair slapped his back rhythmically as he walked. He wore a light beige trench coat, dark blue jeans and a red V-neck t-shirt. He's dark brown skin with icy grey eyes that give daylight something to compliment. Well, technically his eyes are brown, but he wore grey contacts *to catch the right ones* as he put it. I always loved how he'd flip his hair and how he switched his hips so flamboyant as he walked. He has the second-best sashay I've seen in New York.

As he paced back and forth under the tree, my heart felt as though it couldn't beat fast enough. I told him to stay away from my job because his outlandish ways could cost me my part-time position.

Five months into our relationship, he came to my job and told me that we needed to talk. I assumed he just wanted to check up on me since one of my friends with benefits from my teenage years passed away. When I told Johnson how I was feeling about the loss of Patricia while we were outside of my job, he replied, "Oh."

∞

I waited for him to hold me. I anticipated his embrace and encouragement that she was in a better place. He simply made a face.

He stood directly in front of the library entrance until he saw me. Face tighter than up-tight businessman, he glared at me for a few moments.

"Why did you make that post on PicMyBiz about your dead ex-girlfriend? It was unnecessary for you to mention how so-called fine she was. You're with me now. Not her. Do you know how embarrassing it was when my brother saw that? He clowned me and mentioned how bad you got me out here lookin'. The fuck is wrong with you, girl? Also, why you ain't answer your phone? I felt like a small child wearing a clown mask. What do you have to say for yourself?"

I felt my hips cave in and my eyes feel as though they wanted to sink into the back of my head. I didn't want to see myself being exposed to this interaction. I took a deep breath.

"We had history. She's fucking dead. There is nothing to say except to mention how insensitive you're being right now. Fuck how you look to people. A young woman who was once a lover and friend died."

I looked into his eyes, daring for him to respond, stone-hearted. To my surprise, he did.

"Exactly, Roxanne. She's gone. So, why mention that she was fine?"

"Because Patricia was," I retorted.

∞

I shook my head to focus on the present.

My eyes followed him as he paced back and forth by the tree in front of my job. I was curious if this was going to be the same debacle when Patricia passed away.

I texted him back to give me a few moments to head outside. When he saw me approach him, I was greeted with a smile and a sigh of relief.

"What you want, Johnson?"

He reached out to caress my chin, but I blocked his affectionate stroke, and he took a step back.

"You haven't answered my texts, calls and you've been ignoring my e-mails. What's been going on? This is not how we do things. This is why we have so much friction. You won't let me simply love you."

I rolled my eyes and looked away.

"You mean like how I let you love my thighs that you bruised? Or when you loved me to tears by looking at me in disgust just because I like women more?"

He scrunched up his nose, letting his eyebrows cave in and his eyes speak his anger for a few moments. I took a step closer and looked into his eyes. I stood up straight and awaited his reply.

He curled his hands into boxing mode. "There you go again bringing up old shit. Typical, Roxanne."

"I'm calling it how I see it, Johnson. Leave."

I walked away and returned to work.

But he didn't leave.

When I arrived back to my cubicle, three of my coworkers greeted me with grins and busy-bodied winks. The one I talk to the most, Shelly, placed one hand on her hip.

"Your man looks good, girl."

"You can have him," I chuckled.

Me and Shelly worked together for 2 years and I always tried to keep my distance from her. I gave her tidbits about my life because she shared a bit of hers. There was something off about her that I couldn't quite comprehend yet.

"I know ya'll was bickering out there, but relationships aren't perfect."

I looked at Shelly's face for a few moments and winced. I wanted to scream and tell her what he said to me, but she had a point. Relationships aren't perfect.

Everyone bickers and has disagreements. I thought maybe Johnson and I could reconcile. I peeked out my cubicle window and saw him glaring at me. I texted him that we'd talk later on, after I get off work. He texted me back,

I knew you'd come back. I'm glad you came back to your senses. I'll be here when you get off, baby.

During the last few minutes of my shift, Shelly's words played hurricane with my thoughts. She's right. Not all relationships are perfect. I had to make it work. It's not like I had the luxury to bring home a woman. Besides, when things are good between Johnson and me, it's great. But when things are bad, pouring salt on an open wound would be a better option.

When I walked out of the library, Johnson was right where I saw him last, by the tree. As I walked closer to him, his body began to shrink. Gasps from co-workers and bystanders made me want to scream. Johnson was on one knee and beaming. My feet felt as though cement was drying on them.

I couldn't take another step. This can't be happening. We weren't talking for a week. I have bruises on my thighs. Johnson motioned for me to come to him. My stomach was vibrating, and I knew for damn sure that if my coworkers knew what Johnson did to me, their goofy smiles would slide off their faces like heavy rain on windowpanes.

Johnson clenched his teeth and gave me a quick look. Shelly appeared from nowhere and grabbed my hand.

Leading me to him she hollered, "Girl, stop playin' and come get this good man of yours."

When Shelly and I reached him, she stepped to the side. Johnson pulled out a red velvet box from his pocket.

He reached out and held my hand.

"You told me that you wanted a ring, so here you go."

He handed me the box and shrugged. I heard the murmurs and whispers from onlookers. They uttered what I was thinking.

My body wasn't responding. I felt my eyes blink, and I knew there was a lump in my throat. He looked into my eyes and waited for me to open the box. After a few seconds, he grunted.

"So, I get you the ring and now you won't take it?"

Shelly spoke up.

"Put it on her finger, fool. She's just nervous," she yelled out playfully.

People laughed as Johnson snatched the box and fumbled to open it. He shoved the ring on my left ring finger and nodded. He got up with my hand still captured in his and pulled me away from the generating crowd.

"I've got us a hotel to celebrate. Let's get something to eat first."

It was probably the same hotel we always go to on Ebony Avenue.

I seized my hand and surrendered to my gut's demand to resign from moving.

"No, Johnson. I told you that we had to talk."

He yanked my arm, and I flung into his chest.

"We'll talk when we're eating. Don't make me look a fucking idiot out here."

He giggled, then looked back at the crowd and draped his arm over my shoulders.

"Whatever we need to talk about, Roxy, it can wait."

I didn't want another embarrassing confrontation near my workplace, so I marched on with Johnson in silence.

I finally observed the ring. It felt distant. I know it's on my hand, but it feels foreign. The ring belonged to a woman who lost her dignity and didn't know her worth. It must be someone else's. With glimmering side stones, the ring was to be worn by a silly girl trying to keep up an image. A centered yellow canary diamond ring.

He hailed a taxi while I waited on the curb, watching him. His jaw slowly unclenched, and his eyes focused on the passing yellow taxis. I'm sure he'll want me to post the ring on social media. He'll write underneath the description of the picture about how happy I've made him by saying yes.

I watched his foot tap to a rhythm in his head. He huffed at the speeding rejection of filled taxis and would look back at me every now and then. My stomach began to twist again, and my legs were jittery. My heart was tugging to make a run for it, but obligation anchored me to that curb until he grabbed my hand and led me into a taxi.

I shut the door and allowed my knees to succumb to the locked car door.

"Look, I just gave you a ring. What else do you want from me? You know I'm not a bad guy or else you wouldn't be here, Roxy."

It was almost as if a red flag grew out of his mouth.

"I have never done anything, intentionally, to hurt you. I mean let's face it, you're difficult. That masculine persona you have sometimes doesn't help either, but I'm here. I'm still wanting to love you and you won't let me. What's with your attitude right now? I did what you asked, and I paid three months' salary for that damn ring."

He sighed heavily, and his hand slithered up my thigh. Softly, he slinked his hand from my groin to my knee. He took hold of my knee and whispered into my ear while looking at the taxi's rearview mirror.

"Your hissy fits are beginning to piss me off, honestly. The least you can do is show me some respect. Treat your King like the royalty he is, and I won't have to come out of character."

I heard the embarrassment, the yearning to control bouncing from his Adam's apple and onto the roof of his mouth. His ego was filling up the car, and there was barely any room left for me.

I saw it and smiled. I searched his eyes and waited for something to reel me in to make me stay. I found a black hole and a dragon eating away at my reckless hopes of this relationship. Nothing permeated in my chest but rage and shame. I looked at the traffic light two blocks ahead of us. I kissed his forehead and shook my head slowly.

He slid his hand away from my leg and looked ahead.

We stopped at the first traffic light.

I discreetly popped the lock and tapped my big toe.

"So, listen. I was thinking, being that the ring cost a fortune, we can just get married at the courthouse, Roxy."

"I told you, we need to go to at least six marriage counseling sessions before getting married." My eyes were glued to the red on the traffic light.

"All that's unnecessary, Roxy. You love me, I love you. When things get bad, then we'll see a counselor. We communicate well, and as long as we keep talking to each other, we can solve anything."

The light was green, and my heart felt as though it was tapping the tip of my chest.

"That's your problem. You think we're good. You think we're communicating well. We need assistance."

He rolled his eyes and turned his body away from me.

"You're so controlling. You always want things your way. I'm telling you we don't need that counseling shit right now and you're bringing up demands. You know, my mother doesn't even like you. She thought you were too distant when she met you and Dad thinks you're too mouthy and masculine. Yet, here I am trying to spoil you and treat you like a princess. Why do that stupid counseling now?"

The taxi driver and I locked eyes through the rearview mirror. I dropped my eyes, hoping he wouldn't pay too much mind to what was going on.

We reached the second traffic light.

I gripped the door handle, pushed the car door open and got out. Slamming the door behind me, I maneuvered around the various cars waiting for the green light.

I heard Johnson's voice screaming at my back.

"That's not what we do, Roxy!"

I reached the curb and continued walking down the street.

"Roxy! Get back here! Now!"

My heart began to calm down, and I walked a bit slower. If people found out that we were over, what would they say? If it doesn't work with him, I may end up married to a woman. How will I explain that to Mama?

"It's over, baby. Move on."

"Fuck you, then."

I heard the taxi door slam shut as the cars sped by. I twisted the canary ring as I trotted down the city blocks, hoping my heart would stop racing soon.

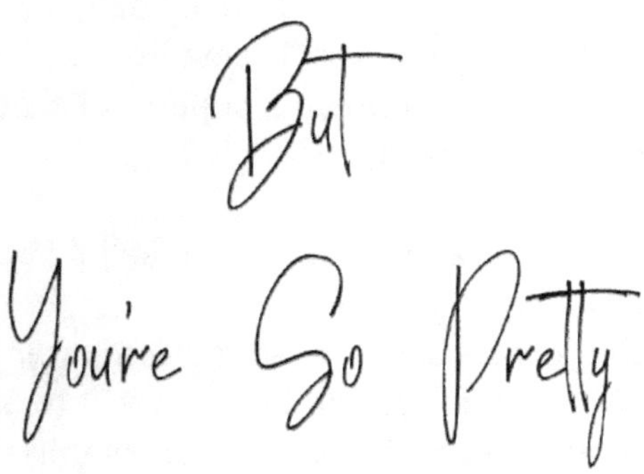

Three days later, Johnson asked for the ring back, and I was happy to return it. I told him to stop by my workplace during my lunch break to pick it up.

When he reached the entrance of my job, a security guard handed him the ring. I received fifteen calls and seven voicemails that lasted five minutes or longer. Each voicemail insisted on how he wanted to talk to me and that he knew we were over. Then he would mention how he was sick of my nonsense and how he would eventually break-up with me if I continue my shenanigans.

Towards the end of my shift, Shelly passed by my cubicle to ask me about the vacation that Johnson and I planned to enjoy March 10th. We booked a round-trip flight to Miami, Florida but hadn't gotten a hotel yet. I balled up my fists and slammed my desk.

"Just when I thought I severed all ties to this motherfucker. I'll send him an e-mail. He was supposed to book a hotel for us this week, but fuck that. I want my half of the money, and that's that," I told Shelly.

"I don't blame you, girl. I remember eaves dropping on your conversation with your supervisor that ya'll were supposed to leave March 10th, right?"

I nodded.

"Okay. Well, call the airline and see if you can get a refund on the flight."

I didn't answer her. I faced my computer and began drafting an e-mail to send to him. Leave it to Shelly to be so damn nosy and eavesdrop. I felt uncomfortable finding out she was eavesdropping, but also relieved. Since she knows, she could read my e-mail to Johnson and tell me what she thinks. Shelly is nosy and makes me iffy at times, but she always felt like the annoying half-sister I never had.

Afternoon Johnson,

You can do whatever you want with that ring. You have given me nastiness and expected me to be okay with it for far too long.

Just a week ago, you placed a ring on my finger, and then moments later, you were talking to me all rude and nasty.

I wanted to talk to you the day you proposed to get to the root of your mean, pompous and EXTRA defensive behavior lately. But, after that taxi ride, I'm done.

From the beginning of this relationship, you pretended to open up. You were so busy trying to protect yourself and make yourself look good, you ended up causing pain to someone you claim you want to be with. I'm hurt and tired. I have no more left in me.

You said things that were below the belt. You disrespected my boundaries. You lied to me countless times. You're so busy checking others, you don't realize how much you need to check yourself. After all these months of me talking about how combative and defensive you are, you finally admitted it. I opened up, attempted to work on my wording, I worked on my over thinking.

I thought things were getting better. But it seems now you think talking to me in any kind of way is okay. You think putting your hands on me is normal. I don't wanna be with you anymore. It's not worth being treated the way you treat me.

I've reached my breaking point. I can't do this anymore. I won't do this anymore

Send me back my $175 via PayPal for the hotel by Monday.

Sincerely, Roxanne

I asked Shelly to read it over.

"I mean it's good, but can't you give it some time? Maybe ya'll can seek counseling? It's complicated with ya'll and besides, I'm sure he sees you eyeing other women when ya'll out. If ya Mama found out that you were eyeing other women, what would she say? I mean I have nothing against you being so free with your sexuality, but you're such a pretty girl, and I'd hate for any good guys to miss out on being with you."

I looked into her eyes and raised an eyebrow.

She continued, "You know what I'm talking about. You do that shit around me too. Does he know, Roxy?"

"I told him that I was bi-sexual but wondering if I just may be a lesbian and he initially flipped, but he knows. He eventually told me that he can change that. I just met the wrong guys. I don't eye other women all the damn time,

Shelly. Besides, it's still no excuse for him to treat me the way he has."

"True. All I'm saying it, there are a few good men out here. I think he's one of them. He's right. Maybe he can change your flaw for loving women. The last thing you want to do is end up with another women and deal with that extra baggage and turmoil. You and your mother would be estranged for sure."

I got up from my chair. Shelly and I were chest to chest for a few moments. She backed up and looked down.

"Then you can have him, Shelly. If you want bruises, lies, disrespect and competition behind closed doors, you have him. By the way, my sexuality has nothing to do with this either."

I turned around and plopped back into my chair. I began to pack up for the day as Shelly stood where I left her.

She finally spoke up.

"Bruises? What bruises? What you mean by disrespect?"

"Forget it, Shelly. Goodnight. I'll see you tomorrow."

I pushed past her and walked down our office's hallway. Waving goodbye to my coworkers, I forced out a grin and tried to pick up the pace.

As I walked out of the entrance door, I breathed in the outside air deeply and looked down at my feet while they guided me to the bus stop. I sat down on the bus bench wincing at the cold metal hitting my bottom.

Across the street from the library there was a park that had weeping willows out front. At the end of the day, I watched the hanging leaves sway from the wind and speedy drivers. But today, I definitely needed to be hypnotized by the rustling trees and green careen.

There was a song buzzing around in my chest. I hummed the tune and closed my eyes, letting the tears fall. I imagined whole notes serenading half notes, while a treble clef played a flute.

What if Shelly is right? Maybe this relationship just needs a counselor to fix us and start over in a good place. Maybe I could convince him to go to at least one counseling session. I felt my phone vibrate in my bag and let my hand dive in the various compartments to retrieve it.

Johnson replied to my email:

Shut up. You will get the money when we meet up tomorrow.

I shoved the phone back into my bag and continued to hum. I was glad that I was on my way to meet up with my best friend.

Stuck Cinderella

Once I arrived at the diner where Annlea and I planned to meet, I scanned the waiting area. I observed various faces smiling, laughing and nodding in acknowledgment to statements. I wanted to scream and interrupt everyone's conversations to remind them that not everyone is good for them. Or maybe I just yearned for their lighthearted conversations and snarky wisecracks. I searched for a seat in the waiting area and found a corner on one of the red bouncy benches near the window. I looked out at the sidewalk, anticipating my best friend's walk. As my right leg anxiously bounced up and down, I thought about my next move with Johnson.

I pulled out my phone and re-read his e-mail response. Everything within me and outwards became a shriveled prune.

I returned my gaze to the window, hoping Annlea would arrive soon.

I needed her input on the matter at hand. She had always been the one in my corner with a sound mind and well-mannered approach to difficult situations. She didn't like Johnson from the beginning and made sure to remind me every chance she had.

She told me a few days ago that she had some good news to share with me. She's been feeling down for the past few months because she's been feeling lonely. Her two closest friends are in relationships, and she doesn't have anyone to kiss at the moment.

She's better off in my opinion. Her beautiful icy green eyes don't need to deal with bullshit from people who claim to love her while acting malicious towards her in private.

I watched people rush down Second Avenue with purpose while others romantically strolled under the sun. I spotted her.

Annlea, five-foot-seven, marching in her brown stilettos, was at the beginning of the block. Her honey brown afro flailed back from the wind, and I'm sure she loved it. Her majestically kinky crown was unapologetic and never assimilated for corporate America. I watched as strangers gawked at her aesthetic while quietly grinning at her tenacity. She never made room for entertaining people's insecurities and her sharp cheekbones were oozing, "Play with me and get served with a good ol' home grown cuss out."

The closer she was to meeting me, the better my posture became. When she spotted me, she stopped, did a quick jig, and speed-walked inside the diner. My body was a rocket as I got up to meet her. She swung open the door, bounced her feet towards me, and wrapped her arms around me. She wasn't fat, nor was she skinny. She was meaty enough for hearty hugs and noticeable curves.

"Roxy, that damn 2 train decided to reroute because someone got sick. Like, why the fuck would they even get on the train knowing their ass is sick?"

Head still nestled in her chest; I was a hyena.

"Good to hear you laughing, Roxy."

I told the hostess that my friend had arrived, and we were seated within minutes. As we shuffled our bags and peeled off our light jackets, we dove into the menu.

Sorting through the items, the e-mail reply sang into my head, and I wanted to play the notes to Annlea. I'm sure she'd dissect the melody and tell me to write another song without giving the previous one any more play. I broke the silence and sighed.

"So, what's the good news, Annlea?"

With her eyes still scanning the menu, she told me about George.

Annlea's cheeks transformed from caramel to rosy red. Her freckles were highlighted from the bashfulness while she looked off into space.

She met him on the Triumph dating website. He's a paralegal in the Bronx. He loves pets and her eyes. He knows his way around the female body.

I nodded as Johnson's e-mail response was pushing to be heard and resolved by her.

Utensils and surrounding chattering filled in the nothingness between us. I didn't want to tell her at the moment what was going on. I strived to stray away from being that friend who always brought some drama to my friends once we fellowshipped. Tears began to fill my eyes, but I refused to be a soap opera character at our favorite diner.

Annlea tilted her head, searching my eyes to find what was troubling me.

I closed my eyes and inhaled, hoping the water in my eyes fell back to where they came.

I pressed my lips to curl into a smile. "Girl, I am so hungry. I just need this food to arrive."

Annlea giggled and agreed.

"Well anyway, Roxy, I saw George yesterday and I'm already missing him something extra serious. I saw him the day before as well."

My face scrunched up.

"Don't you need a break? Like, you just saw the man for two whole days."

Annlea shook her head and rolled her eyes. "That's because I like him. Of course, I want to see him all the time. Don't you like seeing Johnson and miss him once he's gone?"

"No. I actually miss how we saw each other once a week or every two weeks in the beginning. It gave me room to breathe and recharge. Now he Pops up at my job and events, so I see him like every other day. It's annoying honestly."

Annlea stared at me for a few moments and slouched. She gently cocked her head to the side and said, "That's not how you are with your friends. As a matter of fact, you definitely was a fiend for Cynthia. You saw her almost three times a week and had a hissy fit when you only got to see her once a week when her schedule got busy. I remember."

"But ya'll are different, Annlea."

I yanked a napkin from the dispenser and placed it next to my water.

I continued, "Ya'll my friends, and Cynthia is a woman. You know I prefer women. I just need my breaks when it comes to men."

Annlea looked down and mumbled, "Right. You also weren't like that with Kila, Karla, the late Patricia, Samantha and Dawn. Maybe you're just a vagina eater."

I pushed my tongue to the roof of my mouth. I hate when we have this conversation. I've always hated it.

The server was my saving grace as she placed our meals before us.

"I broke up with Johnson via e-mail today."

Annlea dropped her fork and stared at me, wide-eyed and astonished.

"What did he say? Are you okay? What happened?"

She couldn't help but smile, and I had no energy to address that facial response.

I didn't answer her. I pulled out my phone and gave it to her. As she read the e-mail thread, I watched her eyebrows play double-dutch and her mouth squish together. When her face was completely leveled and stoic, I knew she reacted to Johnson's response.

"Yeah," I said.

I watched her finger scroll up to the top of the e-mail thread and read it all over again, searching for some benefit of the doubt to preach to me. I voyaged her eyelids and knew she couldn't find one.

"Get your money and go, Roxy. I already told you this guy wasn't for you. You deserve better and you need to sit down and really reflect on how backwards you've gone."

"Yeah, I know. If he can't electronically send me my money, then he can mail it to me. But meeting up with him will just bring more nonsense."

"I agree, Roxy. But what happened? What made you finally leave him?

I finished chewing a French fry and munched away at the extra words on my mind.

"Well, he proposed to me at my job and—"

"What? Roxy, where's the ring?"

"I had the security guard at my job give it to him a few days later."

You what? Girl, you should've kept that. You could've pawned it or took it to the grave with you. If I were you—"

"But you're not, Annlea."

"I know, but I'm saying if I were—"

"Yet in reality you're not and I returned it to release all ties. Such as my money. I want my money and that's that."

I hate when people tell me what they would've done or what they would've said. Their narrative is their own for a reason. Can't take back the time either. What happened, happened. Annlea knew I hated that.

She sighed and held out her hand for me to hold. "I'm sorry. I just wished you would've reached out to me while this was going on."

"I know, Annlea. I just felt like I was always coming to you about some awful shit he's done to me. I'm just glad it's over and I'm telling you the news now."

She continued to eat her food and nodded.

For the remainder of our time at the diner, we caught each other up about work, life and other mundane things. As we were walking out, my phone vibrated in my back pocket. Annlea opened the door, and I wrapped my arm under hers. We walked up the blocks in silence while I thought about my phone vibrating.

I finally broke the silence, "My phone vibrated, but I'm scared to check it. I don't want no drama today."

"I understand, Roxy. Just know you're gonna have to face that issue eventually."

She's right. Mid-stride, I pulled out my phone and saw a voicemail notification.

I listened to it and with each second, my legs began to feel like boulders:

"I'm getting sick of your shit, Roxy. You're so right about this being over. We will meet up after I am done hanging out with my friends. We'll meet by the R train station at Court Street. Let's settle this once and for all. I'll give you your money in person and we'll go our separate ways. I'm honestly getting really sick of this and I'm losing patience with you. If you keep this up, you are gonna lose me. 5 o'clock, you and me at the Court Street train station."

I stopped walking and pulled Annlea to the side of the sidewalk to avoid random strangers from cursing us out for blocking foot traffic.

"Listen."

I repeated the message and placed my phone to her ear. She held the phone herself, listened, then shook her head and placed her other arm on my shoulder.

She hung up the phone and hugged me.

"You got rid of a psycho," she whispered in my ear.

She released the embrace.

"It's like he feels as though he has the upper hand. It's like he hasn't acknowledged that you broke up with him. The fact that he was threatening how he was going to lose you reveals how he is so used to disrespecting you and your boundaries. You dodged a bullet, Roxy. But, dammit, please don't go back."

I exhaled and let the New York City noise wrap around us. I knew he would turn this break-up into a bedlam.

"I won't, Annlea. I can't."

For the remainder of the day, we shopped around for new books and looked at window displays throughout midtown Manhattan. I set my phone to airplane mode until I arrived home. I refused to allow an ex to ruin my day with my best friend.

I Wont Fold

When I arrived home, I was met with darkness. I walked over to the kitchen and dropped my bags and purse. I smiled at the lingering smell of whatever my mother had made until I heard tapping in the kitchen. Tiptoeing back to my purse, I grabbed my red blade and slid into the kitchen, but saw nothing in the blackness. I flipped the switch on and noticed water leaking from the kitchen light. My neighbor upstairs had a habit of overflooding her bathtub.

Ridiculous. I walked over to my mother's bedroom door and placed my ear to the wood. Searching for noise, I was relieved to only hear the obnoxiously loud fan. I slipped into her room, grabbed my flip flops that were near the closet and put them on. I watched my mother's chest rise and fall peacefully. Her Bible curled under her arm with her glasses still on her face, I knew she probably dozed off while working on a sermon. I slowly pulled off her glasses and placed it on her dresser.

I slid back out of her room and closed the door shut.

"Roxy?" Mama's voice gargled.

"Hey, Mama."

"How is Annlea doing?"

I opened her door and sat on her bed. "She's doing good. She's dating someone new. You good, Mama?"

"I'm blessed and highly favored. Wondering why my daughter don't want to go to church anymore.

Here we go.

"Mama you know I de-converted two years ago. I'm not going back and neither is Annlea."

"Oh, that's right. You gave your heart to the devil. Now look at you. Coming home late, smellin' like alcohol, and I bet those dishes are in the sink."

"Mama, I just got home. I didn't leave any dishes in the sink. Those are your dishes. I only had one margarita at the diner."

Her shoulders rose as she scowled. She interjected and pointed her index finger at me. "Listen here, girl. I don't care who put them dishes in the sink. You see dishes, you wash them."

Her other hand was beginning to ball up waiting for my next reply.

I got up and slammed the door behind me.

"Another reason why you need to go to church. You still sassin' your Mama," she yelled out.

It's as though I'm her black Cinderella. Twenty-two years old and she still thinks I'm some dependent child she needs to boss around.

I peeled off my clothes in the bathroom as quick as I could. I dropped my outfit in the hamper underneath the towel rack. I flipped the bathroom light switch on and closed my eyes. Walking two steps forward, I searched for my heartbeat. Waiting for my heart's rhythm to settle, I heard Johnson's voice in my head.

"Just let a man be a man. Stop fighting me all the time. Why must you always say no?"

I let the tears fall as his voice rained down on my thoughts. At 11:15 at night, there was a flood in my bathroom that left no physical mess, but dammit, was I just as embarrassed. At least my neighbor upstairs and I would have something in common.

"Why must you tell me about your sexuality? I don't care. You're with me. That's all that matters…So what?"

I should've left him sooner. I hated the idea of going public about a relationship only to see it fail with an audience. The various times the red flags waved like ship sails was infinite.

I finally opened my eyes and looked into the mirror. I squinted, then searched for myself within my pupils. I had my Daddy's big eyelids and thick eyebrows. I washed my face and left the bathroom. I peeked back into Mama's room to apologize, and she was asleep again. I went out into the living room and sat on my twin mattress.

I had to admit that I felt lighter and freer knowing I was no longer with Johnson. I dug into my purse to get my phone and jumped back on the bed. I had thirty-seven missed calls and a few text messages. I texted Annlea that I was home, and she replied that she was almost home herself. She lived deep in the Bronx and had to take the #2 train to the last stop, then take a bus for fifteen minutes.

Lost in imagination and visualizing my first sold-out concert in the future, my hand vibrating brought me back to reality.

It was another message from Johnson, but I had time to entertain his foolishness. I wanted my money.

You ain't gettin' shit until you open the damn door.

I read the message in a muttered whisper. This man will stop at nothing to have his way.

There was a bang at the door. I walked over to the door and looked through the peephole. His forehead was wet, and his shoulders were high. I watched him pull out his phone and call me. I tip-toed away from the door and made sure Mama's door was closed. I rushed back out to the living room and answered his call.

"Hello?" I whispered into the phone.

"Open the door, Roxy."

"You're not in control here. Send me my money or you—"

He growled. "Shut up and open this damn door!"

I hung up and plopped on my bed. He wants to have a hissy fit outside my door, so be it. I'm no longer appeasing his outbursts. I'm sick of it. Besides, my apartment building is so used to midnight drama, they probably would just ignore his ass too.

I texted Annlea and my other close friend Maggie. We all were pissed at his shenanigans in the group chat. Fifteen minutes passed and I decided to go to the door and check if he was still there. He was.

I returned to my bed and decided to put on my pajamas. My phone vibrated, and I couldn't help but roll my eyes. It's as though he'd do anything to feel in control. If he doesn't have his way, he will try to force it. Not this time. Nope.

One hand on my hip, I read his message:

You brought this on yourself. You wanted this. You wanted me to be angry. You wanted me to be like this. Here is a $20. I just slid it under the door. Hurry up and pick it up.

My legs took me to the front door, and I placed my hand on the handle ready to curse this bastard out. I can't. He'll have his way. Nope.

I looked down. A twenty-dollar bill was on the floor. I may have to sue this low-life bastard.

For the first time, I wanted to actually spit in someone's face.

I chuckled and Johnson heaved.

"Open this fucking door. Shut up and open it."

I walked over to my Mama's bedroom door and listened for any movements. Once I heard nothing but the fan, I walked past the front door and back to my bed. I pulled my sheet back and slipped under it.

Poor thing really thinks his temper tantrum will be a success. He called me again. I smiled and took a deep breath.

"What now?"

"Shut up and open this door. I'm tired Roxy. This relationship is over."

He doesn't even acknowledge that I broke up with him. Wow.

"Place all the money under the door and leave."

He hung up.

Finally.

I hopped up out of bed, walked over to the door and waited for the other bills to slither inside my home. Staring at the glowing light at the bottom of the door, I became antsy. My phone vibrated once more in my hand. I refused to check it. My eyes still fixated on the light; I began to tap my toes. From my peripheral, I saw red and blue lights fill up the living room.

I finally looked down at my phone and read his message:

Stop repeating yourself. You're such a self-absorbed cheating bitch. I know you're afraid of me.

I strutted to the living room window and peeked through the blinds. There were three cop cars and one angry neighbor from down the hall outside. I guess my neighbors were not a fan of Johnson's shenanigans either. I jolted at the sound of my doorbell and knew who it was. I rushed over to the door and heard their voices. I looked through the peephole and saw a policeman. I opened the door and was met with hazel eyes and folded arms.

"Good morning, ma'am. Can I step inside the home please to get a better understanding of what the noise is about?"

Hell no. I shook my head and replied, "No, but we can speak just like this."

The policeman nodded.

"He was supposed to give me my money. Instead, he showed up uninvited and slid twenty dollars under the door while taunting me along the way. He called me twice since he arrived and was yelling on the phone which I'm guessing is why you guys were called."

"Yes, we received a few calls from the neighbors about a man trespassing and making noise in the hallway."

I nodded. "Yeah, I just want my money."

The cop understood and asked me who Johnson was to me.

I rolled my eyes. "My ex-boyfriend."

He turned to Johnson and asked if he owed me money. He nodded to the officer. He handed the rest of my money over to the officer without glancing at the cop. Johnson's back was against the wall.

He eventually spoke up, "That's all I have, Officer."

"Well, it's allegedly not yours to begin with, am I right?" the officer replied.

With his eyes lowered and his lips softly still, Johnson nodded. His look of defeat made my heart flutter.

The officer handed me the money, and I counted it. I knew that wasn't all Johnson had, but of course he had to make one last attempt to keep my money. My mother came out and asked me what was going on. She walked to the door and saw the policeman. I summarized everything to her and she pulled the door all the way open.

She stared into Johnson's eyes and said, "You ought to be ashamed of yourself. You thought you was gonna have your way actin' like a fool? I know your parents taught you better. You lucky this officer standing here. I'd put hands on you myself."

The cop asked her to allow him to do his job.

"Mama, it's fine. I got this. I'll explain everything to you in full later."

She looked at me for a while and back at the officer. He nodded in agreement with me and she spun around towards her room. She marched to her door and then slammed it behind her.

I didn't press charges, but I asked for a copy of the police report.

Once everyone left and the block was silent, my smile slowly grew until my cheeks ached. There were no more ties to that guy.

I'm free for real.

I sat in Serene's Coffee Shop at a small circular two-seater table next to the window. Whenever life got too heavy or I needed to refocus, I went downtown Brooklyn to Serene's. With my posture perfect and my afro impeccably moisturized; nobody was able to infiltrate my temporary high. I asked a customer—who was seated at a table next to me—to pass me some creamers. I smiled and winked while retrieving three small half and halfs.

I poured the milk in my coffee until it matched the color of my russet-ish complexion. Liquid sugar already in my coffee, I stirred. Watching the warm beverage transform into a light brown color, I thought about what happened two days ago. At what moment did I decide to regurgitate the early morning affirmations and allow a man to spoon feed me words that could shatter my soul?

As the self-evaluating words simmered in my mind to be answered, I stirred faster. Who was I before Johnson? Am I wrong for wanting my money back? Am I messed up for breaking up with him? When I looked up, I was met with aggravated eyebrows and annoyed customers gawking at me. I finally heard the clanging of the spoon banging against the porcelain mug like a pendulum swing. I let go of the spoon.

I looked out the window and watched people pass by the coffee shop in a hurry. New Yorkers rushing to work, school, bodegas, booty calls, and first dates. Anxious to reach point B when we haven't reached point A yet. I wondered what would happen if we all slowed down and really thought about what we wanted in life rather than what we should want. In Mama's eyes, I should want to be a minister like her. She had a dream for me that she's certain is my destiny. A destiny that included being married to a good, godly man that works a 9-5 job. He would also be in ministry, and we'd give her three grandkids.

I wanted none of that.

I wanted something different.

The idea of telling her what I really wanted terrified me. Telling myself out loud made me quiver something bleak. I inhaled for four seconds, held my breath for seven, and exhaled for eight. I repeated the breathing sequence three times and opened my eyes. My album. I haven't created a new song or worked on my album in eight months. I haven't even performed at an open mic for almost a year. Music is my first love.

I looked for my notebook in my purse and opened it to the last page that had lyrics. It was a song about owning your heart's song and letting no one change the lyrics but you.

Ironic.

I heard my name and closed my journal. I saw burgundy boots, dark blue denim jeans and a short burgundy coat. Her smile made me swallow my shock, and I almost forgot my name.

My stunning ex-girlfriend, Karla.

"Hey, Roxy," she said again.

She invited herself to the seat across from me with her smile still glued to her soft face. She shimmied out of her leather jacket, and I watched her breasts shimmy in her burgundy turtleneck sweater.

"I like your outfit. You look warm. Where'd you get those boots?" I stuttered to her as I was eyeing her thick thighs sticking to her jeans like skin on a grape. Her shape was everything that was good in my eyes. Her curves were the sun piercing through the slits of blinds. Eyes like hers were the peanut butter spread on top of celery. Her laughter was like that prideful feeling after completing a passion project.

Her hands blocked my view as she waved near her thighs.

"I'm sure my boots don't stop at my thighs, girl." She winked and continued.

"But anyway, I got these from Jan. She's a playwright that has a boutique up in Harlem. You should check out her shop. I know you'd like some of her stuff."

I smiled and nodded.

Dead air awkwardly settled between us for a few moments until she tapped my notebook.

"I see you still writing songs. Did you finish your album yet, Roxy?"

I wanted our lips to sing to each other, but I knew better to cease entertaining lustful thoughts. Besides, I had Johnson. Wait, I don't have Johnson. I'm free from Johnson. I flashed her a smile.

"Whoa, I guess that album is going well. You're glowing now."

"Nah, I actually haven't written any songs or worked on the album in a long time. But I recently got over certain distractions, so I know I can focus."

"Give me a sec', Roxy."

She got up and went over to the cashier to order something. I knew it was going to be a hot chocolate with three tablespoons of hazelnut syrup. Sweet hot chocolate for sweet Karla.

I remember when we used to meet up at Serene's Coffee Shop, and I ordered for her before she arrived. As much as I missed exploring life and living out mundane moments with her smile in front of me, I knew better. She wanted something serious. She wanted to be with someone who was out about the relationship.

I wasn't ready for all that.

When she returned with her favorite hot beverage in hand, she went straight into it.

"So, how's the love life?"

"Non-existent and satisfying," I replied.

She raised an eyebrow. "So, that means it's complicated and open?"

"No, Karla. I'm single and satisfied to be single."

She sensed my slight agitation and looked down at her hot chocolate.

I hurriedly draped my fingers around her forearm and squeezed two times.

"What about you? I know you have someone. Who's the lucky lady?"

Head still bowed, she smiled. "I'm single and open to rekindle old flames that can burn up all five boroughs."

She's corny like me, and I adored her cheesiness.

"I don't rekindle. If it was burned out, I'll let someone else light it and treat the candle right. Otherwise, we'll burn secretly."

She sighed and looked beyond my head at other customers. I opened my notebook, and she sipped her hot cocoa. I wasn't intimidated by this kind of noiseless language. It was peaceful.

When she finished drinking her hot chocolate, she placed her porcelain mug on the table and yelled, "Oh! I forgot to mention, Jan has a musical coming up, Roxy!"

"Shhhhh, girl you making a public announcement or you just tryna tell me?"

She looked around and shrugged her shoulders. "Anyway, I think you should audition. They just need one person to sing a song about acceptance."

I was down for it, but I needed more information.

"What about acceptance? What's Jan's number? When is the musical? Is it paid? When do—"

"Damn, Roxy. Let me finish." She giggled.

"So anyway," she sang to me, "a song about accepting yourself, I will text you Jan's number. You gotta call her before 6pm though. The audition is this Saturday, and the musical is April 14th. It is paid. Fifty bucks per rehearsal and one hunnit to actually sing on the play date. Anything else, ma'am?"

"Nope. Thanks, Karla. I'll give Jan a call. Maybe this will help me to get back into performing in public again. I need a boost."

"Well, you definitely need to do it then. The world needs to hear that beautiful voice. To be honest, that voice is what made me initially want to get to know you more."

My heart fluttered. She knew what she was doing.

"Yeah, so I'll give her a call. Hey, you have PicMyBiz?"

I retrieved my phone and awaited her response. She looked at me for a few moments and shook her head.

"Of course, I do, Roxy. What's your booster name so I can add you?"

PicMyBiz is a social media website where users can upload images. People can follow other people's pages, comment and like pictures. Over one hundred and seventy-nine million people use PicMyBiz. Surely, twenty-year old Karla would have PicMyBiz. Nevertheless, I wasn't about to go down memory lane with Karla about how we met and what attracted her to me. Nope.

I cleared my throat and readjusted my body. "It's RoxyRoxVocals."

She smiled while searching for my page. Once she clicked the follow button on my page, she showed me her phone. I nodded, and she slid her chair back.

"I better get going. I have work."

I didn't want her to leave.

"Where do you work?

"I work in lower Manhattan."

"Oh, okay. Well, have a good day at work. It was good seeing you again, Karla."

She didn't utter a word. She continued to put on her jacket and rose from her seat.

"Yeah, Roxy. Same."

She walked out the door.

A song about acceptance. That's interesting, I guess.

I logged into my PicMyBiz account and scrolled through the pictures of other users that I followed.

A picture caught my eye, and my heart began to race as I read the caption. Johnson is really good at saving his public persona even when no one is trying to attack him.

As I held the table to brace myself, I clicked on his page and viewed the most recent photos he uploaded. The third photo was a picture of a police cop and a police officer writing in a note pad. Underneath the picture the caption read, *she called the police on me. All I did was love her with all my heart.*

My fingertips gripped the edge of the table tightly. I wanted to flip that round table and scream. I clicked on the next photo. It was a picture of himself looking up at the sun with his eyes closed. A tear was falling down his face. The caption read, *I forgive you and I love you still.* I placed my phone on the table and sat very still.

I took a screenshot of our whole conversation from that night and left Serene's Coffee Shop.

When I arrived home, I uploaded the screenshots on PicMyBiz and turned off the comment section. No need for a discussion about his actions. Just need to clear my name and set the record straight. He wants to show out, fine. I'll show both our asses and gloss it too.

Voila, bitch. Voila.

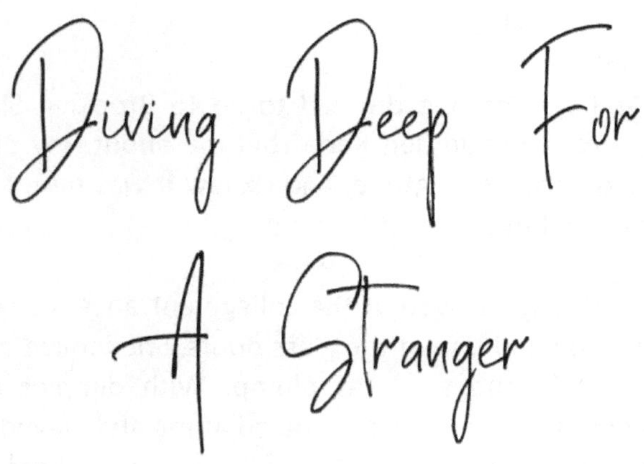

I was itching for Saturday to arrive. Once Johnson's friends saw my screenshots and asked questions, he took his last two pictures down from PicMyBiz. A few people texted me and called to see if I was okay. It just felt good putting Grandma's timeless advice to use: Always keep your receipts.

I told Mama the day after everything happened, and she scolded me for not waking her up. I wanted to handle it myself. And I had.

I let her read his text messages and watched her shake her head slowly. "Hmph," she replied after reading the messages.

"I just hope you actually stay away from him. You grown, but don't be foolish, Roxanne. I know for sure he ain't allowed to step foot in this house. This is why you need to be in prayer so you can see these things coming. Give it some time. He may come around. His parents raised him well by raising him to know the Lord."

"He's outta my life for good. I'm not giving it any time."

She chuckled.

I left it alone.

As I was getting dressed to go to Brooklyn Sienna College for the audition Karla told me about, my phone sang a distinctive ringtone, and I knew it was him. I let it ring as I continued to get dressed.

∞

When I arrived at the college entrance, I saw Jan standing behind one of the glass doors. She looked about six feet tall, and she was plump. With dimples deep enough to take a nap in, she smiled at me and waved. She swung the door open and yelled, "Roxanne, hurry up. You're the only one who came to this audition. I really hope you can sing."

"I can sing with the grace of three walruses if that's what you're asking," I joked.

"Aight cool, Roxanne" Jan replied.

She motioned for me to follow her up the escalator and down a hallway.

Jan stopped in front of a door, opened it, and let me inside first. I was greeted by a sea of glares and curious faces. The conversation continued as Jan looked for a chair. There were fifteen people seated in a circle. An old red piano occupied the left side of the room, and a mirror took over an entire wall on the right side. My heart raced, and I suddenly felt small enough to fit in Jan's pocket. Shrinking would be a good idea right about now. I would climb in Jan's front pocket and call it a good life.

Jan clapped her hands twice, took a deep breath and exclaimed, "Alright, ya'll, alright. We got Roxy who was supposed to be auditioning to replace Deon's spot, but being that she's the only one..."

The group laughed.

"Well, yeah. So, we gonna see what she got and then continue."

They all scooted back a little waiting for me to enter the middle of the circle, but I couldn't move. My legs were rubber, and I was sure clear critters were creeping up my hips.

Jan whispered into my ear, "Go ahead and sing the song I e-mailed you on Thursday night. My people don't bite. Go ahead."

She gently pressed her hand on my back, and I held my breath.

I walked to the middle of the circle and finally exhaled.

I heard murmurs about me being too stuck up to say hello, how I looked shy and bourgeoisie. I was trying to sing without throwing up my guts on everyone.

I released a half grin and closed my eyes. I sang from my belly. I rolled out the memorized lyrics I rehearsed for three hours a day off my tongue. A song well-rehearsed tastes good when you finally perform it. When I was finished, I heard nothing but a truck hitting a pothole outside. Suddenly, everyone slid back, put their food away and placed their chairs to the back of the room.

Jan finally spoke up, "Alight, ya'll, let's get back to scene eight. Sarai, make sure you walk a bit slower so people won't be distracted during Tony's number."

I tapped Jan on the shoulder and asked her if I got the part. She nodded and told me to watch the rehearsal today. She handed me a script mentioning that my part is during the first act, scene five. One song and that was it. Thank goodness.

I sat towards the door and watched as everyone sang, acted, and cackled at forgotten lines. During break time, I sat in the hallway with one of the other actresses who only had one song to sing as well. She was thin, dark brown skin with a red wig that stopped at her butt. She had light green contacts and matching green nails. Her eyes were magnetic. I could tell she could easily draw anyone into her.

"So, how'd you find out about this play?" she asked.

"Oh, an old flame told me about it and connected me with Jan. How about you?'

She munched away at her chips for a few moments. "I've been in this from the beginning. Jan and I have been friends for years. She wrote an ad on her website that she was doing auditions for her play, and I was interested. So, I went to the audition and got the part."

"Oh, okay. That's cool."

She paused chewing and giggled to herself. Another actor joined us in the hallway and waved at me.

"Hey, what's your name again? I'm sorry, I was really trying to focus on my lines in there."

"Roxanne, but I prefer Roxy. Yeah, you did good. Your character is very concupiscent, and you and Audrey executed your roles well. What's your name?'

He stuck out his chest and sat on the bench across from me. "My name is Tony. I like your smile and style. Like, it's easy to see you're nice and you don't have anything to prove to anyone."

"I don't, Tony. Not a damn thing." I giggled.

He laughed with me and said, "Shit, me neither."

The actress with fiery red hair interjected. "You know you're only here because you are replacing someone right?"

Tony swallowed his laughter and shot a look at her.

"No, I didn't. But either way, I'm here and I'm going to be in the play right along with you. And who are you?" I asked.

She began to tap her foot. "My name is Deena, and I think you should—"

Audrey ran out of the rehearsal room and slid right next to me. "Hey, Roxy, your voice is spectacular! You're a natural songbird, you know?"

"Thanks, Audrey. I was just telling Tony how you two executed your scenes well."

"Well, thanks, Boo. But you don't have to flatter Tony. We all know I was the best during those scenes."

Tony shook his head and waved her off. "Please, I was a beast in that room," he shot back.

We all laughed except for Deena. She was still eyeing me, and I refused to give her any attention. She finally sat down beside Tony and slid two of her fingers in between his braids. He nervously smiled and ducked his head away from her green claws.

"What's wrong? You don't want nobody to touch your hair, Tony?" she asked.

"No, I just don't want you touching it," Tony shot back.

Audrey snickered and turned towards me. "So, you got any music out or anything, Roxy?"

My chest felt as though little worms were playing tag on top of it as I thought about what Johnson did during the first and last time, I was in a recording studio.

He kept stopping the producer and the engineer from recording me every few lines that I sang. He would tap the glass and motion his hand for me to stop singing. He would tell the engineer how I should do it over because my voice was not good enough or that my note was not clean enough. The engineer would scold him and tell him my voice was fine. That was the last time I sang in front of anyone.

I shook my head. "No, not yet, but I have a few songs I'd like to record soon. What about you, Audrey?"

She frowned, sucking her lips in. She shook her head wildly enough for me to hear her beads that wrapped around the ends of her box braids.

"I'm a lawyer. This is just something I like to do every now and then. I'm not really an artist. I'm doing Jan a favor, really."

"Mm."

"So, what are your songs about?" she asked as she plucked her phone from her jean skirt pocket.

"Mainly about my love life, finding my inner voice and learning to be more confident in myself."

She flashed a smile as she scrolled through her phone. "That's great," she replied, her eyes shooting back and forth at her phone's screen.

"Have you been to a recording studio yet?"

Before I could answer, another person exited the rehearsal and everything within me felt settled.

She glided past me and stood in a corner diagonally from me. She had a perfectly plucked afro that crowned her. She flashed a dimple to us before she glued her eyes to her phone. The bottom of her dark baggy jeans neatly covered the tongue of her maroon and black sneakers that screamed a street suave I wanted to get close to. Something within me wanted to leap from the bench and interview her to be in a major role in my life until fin was written across my eyelids.

Who the fuck was this person?

Audrey tapped my knee nabbing my attention away from the mystery being. I jolted back and replied, "Oh, yes. I have been to a studio, but my ex-boyfriend was an ass. I haven't been to one since anyway because they can be so expensive yet the quality of the work is subpar. Like, I'll pay three-hundred fifty dollars for a two-hour session with the engineer. Then pay another two hundred to mix two songs, only to receive lackluster mixing and a few muffled moments on the track. Nope, nope, nope."

Audrey shrieked in giggles. "Girl, I've heard stories. My cousin paid five thousand dollars for a studio to record, mix and finish their album. She said that she should've done it herself."

"You know there is a great studio on fifty-seventh street and Lennox. You get what you pay for. Quality sound and professionalism. One of the actors who was in my documentary recommended me," the mystery person inserted.

I finally saw her big, brown eyes and I wanted to know everything about her. I was sure I was slowly melting every second I spent staring into them. Our eyes played freeze tag until Audrey spoke up.

"Yes, Showla Studios. I heard of them. They don't advertise much. Roxy, this is Silk."

Her deep brown complexion probably felt like silk too.

All of my teeth wanted to take a peek at Silk as I flashed her a smile and waved.

"Hey, Silk."

"Hey, Roxy. Nice voice you got there. I love the sultry vibe that lingers when you sing. I hope you record soon."

I'd sing for her anytime. "Thanks, Silk. What's the name of the documentary you did?"

She dropped her phone in a pocket inside her jacket. My eyes followed her every move. She walked three steps towards me and smiled.

I was definitely melting.

She tilted her head to the side. "It's called *Choices.* It came out last year, and Jan actually helped me on set."

"Yes, I heard about your little documentary," Deena chimed in.

Everyone sighed and rolled their eyes, except for Silk. She chuckled for a few moments and shook her head.

"Damn, Shawty. That green is lookin' really good on you. The hair and nails."

Deena flipped her hair back and smacked her lips. "Yes, I know right?" she replied.

Silk spoke calmly, "It matches your insides. That little documentary won three awards, and your man still raves to me about it. But yeah, you keep rockin' that green you wearing inside and out."

Tony was cackling. "Finally, somebody put your miserable, jealous ass on blast."

Deena rolled her eyes and stomped away while mumbling, "I was simply being honest. It was small to me." She walked down the hallway to the elevator.

Tony asked Audrey about their scene, and she turned her back to me and engaged with Tony as if we were not conversing a few moments earlier.

"Okay," I said aloud.

Smooth tongued and chill, Silk sat next to me, and I was sure that in a few more moments, my entire being would be in a puddle.

"She and Tony are really close. Don't take it too personal. She's an authentic soul." Silk nudged me with her elbow.

All I could do was grin. My mind was going in nine different places, searching for something interesting to say.

"So, where you from, Roxy?"

"Seven. I mean, yellow. Brooklyn. I'm from Brooklyn."

Where the hell did, I get the number seven from? Now she's going to think I'm deranged. I need to shrink now.

She surprisingly laughed and replied, "I'm from eight. I mean Harlem. I'm from Harlem. You have a beautiful voice. Is there anyone—"

Jan called us back inside to continue rehearsing and I wanted to chop her in the throat for disrupting Silk's response.

∞

When I arrived home, I called Annlea and updated her about my first day at rehearsal. I didn't mention Silk. I couldn't. Annlea picked up on my voice being a bit chipper than usual though.

"What else happened at this rehearsal? You found twenty dollars on the floor? Why you extra perky today?"

I held my breath for a moment, ready to confess my arbitrary feelings for a stranger.

"Um, hello? Roxy, I know you heard me, girl."

I exhaled and forced, "Can't a girl just be happy with life? Damn."

"Of course, she can, Boo. But I know you're full of shit right now and hiding something. But I'll be here when you're ready to spill it. How you doing after breaking up with that clown?"

I clenched my jaw and chewed up every foul word I had to say about Johnson. "I'm fine. Honestly though, I feel as though he'll never take responsibility for his actions, and that pisses me off. What bothers me the most is how his sister had the nerve to comment under one of his slander pictures of me on PicMyBiz. She commented that she's so glad he got rid of me because I'm a bully. Meanwhile—"

"Wait, hold up. What? She called *you* the bully?"

"Yes, Boo. She called me the bully. Meanwhile, this fool has attempted to manipulate me into silence, put his hands on me, belittled me, and every time I placed a personal boundary, he disrespected it."

I wasn't done yet. My belly was tumbling aches and hurts from that man. It was all coming up, and I couldn't help it. I paused and waited for Annlea to chime in.

"Sorry, Annlea. I'm just so pissed. That relationship was exhausting and draining. Like he really tried to keep up this image like we were perfect when he was treating me like crap and refusing to fess up to it."

She said, "Roxanne, don't you ever apologize for speaking on the hurt. That's a part of the healing process. You have been ignoring my calls, and you haven't called me since the incident with that fool showing up at your house and causing a scene."

I chimed in, "You're right, Annlea and I should have—"

She cut me off and continued, "Oh, no you don't. Listen, we all respond to life's curveballs and fuckery differently. I am not trying to attack you, Roxanne. I want you to know that as your best friend, you ain't never hold stuff in. So, for you to hold certain parts of that relationship in, it must have done some damage. Have you thought about seeing a counselor to help you through this?"

I love Annlea. She'd always been supportive but kept it real with me.

"Well, the police officer mentioned some place called Safe Haven on Court Street, Downtown Brooklyn. I don't know though. I have work and—"

"Nope. Not having it. Your job is only a ten-minute bus ride from downtown Brooklyn. Matter of fact, hold off on that money excuse if that was going to be your next response because you have a police report. At Safe Haven, the first six sessions are either free or low cost, when you have a domestic violence police report. So, what's up? You want me to come with you to schedule?"

I knew I wanted to go to counseling. Being that it would be free for me. I had to take the offer. I actually felt excited once she mentioned a counselor. The last time I had a counseling session was in high school. Mama made me see a Christian therapist because she read a page in my diary about having a crush on a girl in my math class. That therapist kindly told Mama that nothing was wrong with me. Mama made me stop going.

"Alright. I'll go. But you gotta meet me after work."

She agreed.

She hung up after her boss caught her talking on the phone at her desk.

I plopped on my bed and looked at the chipped paint above me. It appeared as if the ceiling were about to crack open and all my neighbors' furniture would come tumbling down.

I watched my belly rise and fall as I took deep breaths. The apartment was quiet. I envisioned Silk's chest rising and falling. Her lips speaking with conviction and peace. Mama was at an evening church service and the neighbors upstairs barely made a sound. I thought about the various text messages and instant messages I'd received from people who saw my screenshots I posted on PicMyBiz.

I appreciated them checking on me, but I was also a little embarrassed. A few people felt as though I shouldn't have done that. Some people felt as though I should have kept it to myself. To simply swallow my narrative and look like the ceiling above. I refused to hold it in anymore. I refused to have any more cracks in my life due to a voice fighting to break free.

I closed my eyes and reminisced on when he would sashay down 14th street and Union Square and flip his hair. I couldn't help but chuckle at his flamboyancy. I remember how he didn't look back to his side to see if I was there until at least thirty steps later. I would randomly stop and just watch him walk ahead. He rarely noticed that I was no longer walking by his side.

I shook away the thought and undressed.

I had to get away for a while. I remembered that I technically had a trip to Miami still booked from the money I saved up and the money Johnson gave back to me. I'm still going to Miami, just as a single lady now.

I called Maggie and Annlea and told them what I planned to do. They offered to put their money together so they could bump me to first class. All I needed in life was my support system and my music.

Dancing With Dr. Ramsey

Safe Haven was a non-profit organization for victims of domestic violence. With five floors, it housed four on-site counselors, three social workers, a retired domestic violence detective, and nine emergency shelter rooms for those who have been battered.

It was a mad house when Annlea and I set up my first appointment. Due to my police report from Johnson pulling up to my house, the first six sessions were free. My thirteen-dollar per hour income definitely helped in that arena as well. My counselor's name was Dr. Ramsey, and she had eyelashes long enough to cool down the entire city of New York on a hot August day.

Other than Annlea, my Daddy was the only one who knew that I sought a counselor. He was completely supportive and excited for me. I'm sure if I told Mama, she would've felt as though I didn't need it. I eventually texted Mama right before I left Safe Haven to let her know that I was going to begin counseling sessions soon. She wished me luck. After I officially set up my appointment, I hugged Annlea, and we went our separate ways. I walked over to the B68 bus stop and joined the other cold folk anticipating the bus.

I wondered if Johnson moved on and found a girlfriend already. I wanted to know if he told his family what he did to me. The bus arrived and it was surprisingly empty. I snagged a seat in the back and watched the bus roll down the winter streets of Brooklyn.

∞

I took a day off to attend my first session with Dr. Ramsey. When I reached Safe Haven, I stood in front of the glass double doors for a few seconds. I watched the condensation fog up the glass as I breathed on it and waited for something to tell me to go home. Nothing happened. I took a deep breath and pulled the door open. I was met with sweltering heat and the click-clacks of three women walking outside. I took the elevator to the second floor where all the counselors were, and I sped up to the front desk.

The receptionist asked for my name and told me to have a seat. I sat across from a man who had a blackened eye and his leg bounced. I closed my eyes and listened to the heel of his shoes consistently tapping the rug. There was bossa nova jazz playing in the waiting area and two huge windows that gave the sunshine room to intrude the blank spaces of the offices. I squinted from the sun's rays but embraced the warmth as I shimmied out of my coat. A woman and her friend sat in the waiting area with a dog that silently wagged its tail.

My eyes jolted open when the phone rang. The receptionist spoke in a whisper, then hung up. I felt my

63

body settle into the chair. I heard heels click-clack down a hallway and I knew it was Dr. Ramsey.

"Ms. Patterson?" she declared at the front desk.

I held up my finger and smiled. I picked up my things and walked up to her. She returned the smile and told me to follow her.

Her office was huge. There was a purple couch, a yellow chic love seat, a round purple carpet, and three bookshelves that stood against the wall. A large window with a man outside cleaning the panes loomed across the side wall.

There was a small lonely yellow stool next to the purple couch. I placed my coat and bag on the stool. I watched her sit on the yellow love seat with a notepad and red pen. She invited me to have a seat on the purple couch, and I dropped my body, sinking into the leather and scooting back until comfortable.

I wondered how many people had napped on this couch.

"So, how are you, Roxanne?"

"You can call me, Roxy, Dr. Ramsey."

"Okay."

"So, you married, Dr. Ramsey?"

"Well, this session is about you, but yes, Roxy. I've been married for fifteen years."

She continued, "You told me during our intro meet with your friend, Annlea, that you just broke up with your boyfriend?"

I nodded.

She smiled. "So, how did you and your ex-boyfriend meet?"

I couldn't help but roll my eyes when she asked that question. I wish Karla's mother never introduced me to Johnson, but I know she had good intentions.

"I met him in church. My ex-girlfriend's mother introduced me to him. His church visited my former church for Men's Day service. Johnson's father preached during the afternoon service. He was on the praise and worship team. I sing too, so my ex-girlfriend's mom thought we should get to know each other," I replied

Now that's over with, let's move on.

She didn't. She wanted more details. Maybe I shouldn't have come here. I thought this was supposed to be my place to vent and that's all.

"So, you two hit it off from there?" she asked.

I couldn't help but kiss my teeth.

"No. About a year later, I saw him again at an open mic night. We exchanged numbers, went on a date and the rest is history. I wish I never met him, and I hope he rots in misery." My leg began to bounce as I continued.

"Even from the beginning there were signs I should've left his ass alone. Like on our first date, he walked ahead of me. I went down to tie my shoe, and he didn't realize that I wasn't walking with him until we got to the end of the block. Or the fact that he was rude to the server at the restaurant we ate at during our first date. And you know what, Dr. Ramsey?"

Face unmoved she said, "No, what?"

I felt my chest rumble as my leg caressed the couch vigorously.

"He doesn't like when he doesn't get all of the spotlight. It's like, all of a sudden, he has this impulsive hissy fit and expects me to linger behind my own shadow for his comfort and fragile ego. It's disgusting. He's shaped like a box. I like the way he flips his hair and the way he switches when he walks, but he doesn't have curves. There isn't a soft, welcoming vibe to him. There is this scent that he has, well, all men have. Damn it it's repulsive. Why do we women tolerate that smell? It's like they all have it. Like my ex-girlfriends all had various smells, but I was always lured in by them, not turned off."

I couldn't stop talking. I didn't mind. The more I talked the lighter I felt. The more my lips moved, the tightness in my stomach loosened.

She interjected,

"Can you give me an example of a time he acted impulsively due to a lack of attention?"

"It wasn't lack of attention. He needed to have all of the attention," I corrected.

She nodded quickly. "Okay. I hear you. What's the first example of a time he acted impulsively due to a need for all the attention?"

That was an easy question. The only problem was actually saying it. My lips were ice. I felt as though my tongue wrapped around my tonsils and my mouth was shut.

"Roxy?" she said as she tilted her head. Her short hair dangled in the air and my lips began to thaw out.

A flashback of Johnson's fingers wrapped around my neck glitched in my head like a 1940s cinema film. I remember his eyes appeared as though his soul had vanished within his body. His pupils were wide as he clenched his jaw.

"Roxanne." I felt the couch cushion next to me sink in.

"Oh. Yes, one time Johnson and I were at this dance hall, and he was mad that the DJ asked me to do a line dance on the stage," I said.

"Okay. What did he say after you finished dancing on stage?" she asked.

"It doesn't matter. I had a good time, and he had a hissy fit about it. But I let him have it."

She walked back over to the love seat, picked up her notepad and sat down.

She nodded and looked into my eyes. "What made you think about that example first, Roxanne?"

"I don't know," I responded. I shrugged as my leg began to bounce again.

"Well, did you have a good time dancing?" she asked with a smile.

I nodded and examined a bird flying past the window.

I inhaled, closed my eyes. "Too bad he choked me for it."

I never said it so plainly. I never said it aloud for that matter.

Dr. Ramsey's pen began to move, and I sat up. My heart felt as though it was sliding in my stomach. I have to fix this quick.

"But that's only because he was ignored often as a child. His problem is, he has to be seen all the time to make up for all the time he was being ignored. He vowed to never be ignored or rejected again. He's come a long way."

She nodded as she continued to scribble.

"I did stop talking to him for a while after that. He apologized and told me how he was bullied in high school and how he was often rejected by people. He is still dealing with that, you know. Are you going to speak to my mother about this? Will you tell her about the women thing and the men smell thing?"

Her pen did the talking, but I needed her lips to move. She needed to say something. Is she judging me? Will she report that situation at the night club to the police? Is she writing me a prescription?

When her pen stopped, she looked into my eyes and said, "Everything that you mention in this room stays in this room, unless you have a suicide plan or a plan to hurt someone. You are also a legal adult. Your mother, or anyone else for that matter, will not be informed of what you have told me. Now, when did you begin to speak with him again?"

I was attempting to interpret her eyes so I could answer properly, but all I saw was a blank canvas with neutral tones on a palate.

"I'm done with this session. I don't know what you're going to do with my business," I replied.

I rose quickly from the couch and slid my hand underneath the inside my coat. I scooped it up and flung it over my shoulder. I'll just use my songwriting as therapy.

I marched towards the door and thought about my upcoming vacation. I don't need a therapist judging me and telling me what to do. I need air, peace, and a fresh scene for a while.

Dr. Ramsey stood up with me and scribbled even faster. Notepad still holding her eyes captives, she spoke softly,

"Roxanne, trust isn't always given from the start. I'm here to listen and help. If it takes time for you to open up, that's okay. I want you to have what I'm writing in my notes."

What in the world? All of this time, I thought she had been writing stupid notes about me and doodles while I was peeling open my heart. This woman is something else.

I took her little note, though.

I spun around and allowed my eyebrows to cave in. I rolled my eyes and waited for her next move.

She ceased writing, ripped the note from her pad and folded it. She walked over to me and smiled. "Listen, I'm here when you're ready, Roxy."

She opened the door for me as I took the note from her fingers.

I didn't say a word. I walked out the office, strolled past the receptionist desk and waited for the next elevator.

Once I was out of the entire building, I opened the note and read it.

Roxy, please remember these six important things
- If you return to him, it's okay to seek help.
- You cannot help who you're attracted to.
- Research pheromones.
- The desire to hide what really happened in your relationship with Johnson is okay, but counterproductive towards healing and moving forward.
- Feeling guilt and shame about what he did to you is normal, but it isn't justified.
- Lastly, the abuse is not your fault.

When you're ready, call anytime to make an appointment!
- Dr. Ramsey.

I crumpled up her note and shoved it into my coat. I headed to the bus stop to go back home and get ready for my vacation.

Getting To Know Her

With everything that happened, the idea of sitting in a fancy seating section made me sit up straight on the bus. I sipped my tea with my pinky up. I would walk with my head held high down any block my feet touched. I felt supported. During one of our rehearsals, Silk invited me to an open mic that she would be featuring in. I asked her what she would be doing. She simply flashed a smile.

"Show up and find out, lil' lady."

Of course, I accepted the invitation. We exchanged numbers that same rehearsal, and I texted her once I arrived home to wish her well. She replied back:

You too lil' lady.

She called me lil' lady. I vowed to myself to never to text her again. What if she thinks I like her? I don't need her knowing that I have feelings for her. Every time she called me "Lil' Lady" my heart felt settled. I attempted to suck in my mouth to hide the smile.

Three days before my trip to Miami, I scurried around my house searching for an outfit to wear to Silk's feature. I bounced between my storage bin in the living room and the armoire in my mother's bedroom. I had seven hours until I had to leave my house for her show.

I decided to wear a pair of my black slacks and a pink buttoned-down silk top. I styled my hair into two corn braids and wore black and pink hoop earrings.

I hope she likes my outfit. What if she brings her girlfriend? I know I said I wouldn't text her, but I should text her and ask if she's bringing a romantic partner. Does she even have a girlfriend?

I grabbed the iron from the kitchen and looked at it for a while. The last time I ironed anything was for the job interview for the library that I work at now. I don't want her to think I like her or anything. I don't have the energy to be rejected by someone I like right now. I don't know if she's even in a relationship.

I shook the questions out of my head and walked over to my suitcase that was already packed for Miami. I don't know what's in store for me there, but for damn sure: I will have a good time.

I called Annlea and Maggie via three-way. I told them about Silk inviting me to an open mic show that she'll be featuring at.

"Remember, Roxy. You're single. I know you just broke up with that devil, but remember: you're single," Maggie replied, her voice softer than clean sheets blowing in the wind on a summer day. She knows I would still move as if I was in a relationship post break-up.

I brought my phone into the bathroom as I listened to Annlea and Maggie fuss about what would happen if Silk actually had feelings for me. I looked into the mirror and everything within me paused. My cheekbones were visible. I looked down at my legs that were evidently smaller than usual. When did this happen?

I chimed in their bickering and said, "Hey, I lost a lot of weight, ya'll."

Annlea sucked her teeth and Maggie mumbled her frustrations.

"What? Am I missing something? When did I start losing weight? That's probably why some of my clothes weren't fitting. I just thought they were becoming worn or stretched out."

I heard fuzz and background noise flooding my ear for a few moments.

I broke the silence with my eyes still gazing on my new-found body.

"Um, is anyone going to answer me? You two have seen me, and I know ya'll seen the change."

Annlea spoke up. "Yeah, we noticed. The first time I told you that you lost weight, you just shrugged me off and told me that you lost weight in the winter. Then when Maggie told you, you denied it. The second time I told you, you told me that you were just stressed and to leave it alone.

"I was going to tell you that I was concerned, but Johnson chimed in and claimed that you were the same beautiful woman he saw when he first met you. You don't remember when me and him ended up arguing after that? 'Cause that's when he accused me being jealous of him and you had to break us up."

Maggie butted in, "How in the world did he place himself in that situation? Why would you be jealous of him when you were talking about Roxy's brand spanking new skimpy tree body?"

Annlea replied, "Girl, I don't know. Self-centered fool told me that my comment about my friend's weight loss was a jab at how he looked. I don't know how that makes sense, but it came out of his mouth as though he was declaring the cure for cancer."

As they bickered about my ex, water blanketed over my eyes and my body looked like a swaying pipe cleaner.

I asked aloud, "Where did I go?"

Hot streams rolled down my cheeks as the weight of what I allowed in that relationship dug into my shoulders. A plethora of moments that I knew I should have walked away from Johnson for, pushed me down to my knees. The times I surrendered goals to his ego wailed from my mouth. My friends ceased talking and listened to my lamentations. Like an idiot, I handed Johnson the version of myself that was blossoming into a woman I dreamed of. I gave it to him, and he gobbled it up hoping his own shadow would shine brighter than my own.

I asked again, "Where did I go?"

Maggie finally answered me. "You went to a place you felt you had shrunken yourself for someone. Thankfully you're not there anymore, Roxy."

I wanted to answer her, but the words couldn't get past the ache that roofed the bottom of my larynx.

After twenty minutes, I was undressed, cried out and holding the phone to my ear faithfully listening to the silence on the other end.

"Roxanne, you out of it. Continue to cry when you need to. Go enjoy yourself tonight at Silk's event. Try to be present. What happened in that relationship has happened. So, enjoy what's going to happen today, what's going to happen tomorrow when you hang with us, and what will happen in three days while you're in Miami."

I nodded and agreed. I hung up, looked in the mirror one last time and got into the shower.

∞

On my way to the venue, it felt as though little butterflies were tickling the bottom of my belly in the taxi. I tried to look out the window and watch people whiz by. My mind was racing with what if questions, and I entertained every last one until the car completely stopped and the driver was yelling, "Ma'am. Ma'am, we are here. You pay now."

I circled two fingers in my pocket until I felt the twenty-dollar bill and slid it out. As I waited for him to give me my change, I observed the outside of the venue. It was a small bar with obnoxious white and red lighting. "11:11 Bar and Lounge" lit up the sidewalk, and I was ready to go back home.

"You don't want change?" the driver said with frustration swimming on his tongue.

I nodded feverously and apologized. I snatched the change, tumbled quickly out of the taxi and slammed the door. I walked up to the venue and looked up at the lights. I felt the heat overcast my face as I breathed slowly until my nerves felt safe enough to settle in. I tapped my back pocket to feel my phone and I pulled it out. I read the time aloud and looked around.

"6:45pm. I'm early."

I pulled open the glass door and slipped inside.

It was intimate. Twelve square tables lined up on the left and a bar on the right where two guys were cackling. One lady slurring her words over the phone at a table, and me, standing in front of the door. Silk was nowhere to be found, and I was relieved. I walked over to the bar and jumped on one of the stools. The bartender walked over to me with a smile, and his hands plastered on the table.

"Hey. What's your tongue feeling for?" he asked.

"Um. I'd like a cranberry and vodka for now. Can I see a menu?"

He nodded and handed me a small, laminated pamphlet from his pocket. As I skimmed over the list of foods and drinks, I soothed myself to the sounds of the clanging glasses and water from the bartender.

I knitted my brows as I searched for something to scarf down my throat until Silk arrived. I decided to order the macaroni and cheese with bacon bits. I waved my hand up and the bartender walked over.

I felt a gentle touch on my back.

"Hey Lil' Lady. What's up?"

I turned to my right and was met with Silk's beautiful brown eyes and that smile I'd risk it all for. I was waiting for the butterflies to terrorize my chest and my hands to sweat. As she wrapped her arm around me to give me a side hug, I wanted more.

I knew I had to wait. I didn't know if someone would be behind her with eyes that spoke of having Silk's heart. I looked and saw no one.

"I'm out here solo, Lil' Lady. How you doin'?"

"I'm good. I arrived mad early," I replied.

I tried everything I could to cease beaming. My lips, teeth and gums betrayed my request to stop grinning as though Santa came early.

"It's okay. I'm always an early bird myself. What time you get here?" she asked as she sat on a stool right beside me.

"6:45."

The bartender placed my drink in front of me and took Silk's and I's food order. She offered to pay for my meal as a thank you for attending her show. It was quiet for a few moments, but I didn't mind it and neither did she. Her scent was alluring and all I could do was wonder what it would be like to be under her in a room. With her hair styled in corn rows, I gazed at the ends of her braids stopping at the bottom of her back. She had on a blue bomber jacket, but I knew she was curvy.

She noticed me looking and chuckled.

"I know you're probably wondering why I still have this jacket on. It's a habit of mine," she spoke up.

Realizing my jacket was still on, I smiled and said, "Yeah, me too."

I shimmied out of my jacket and sat on it.

As time went by, we spoke about where we grew up, if we went to college and what time she was set to perform. She'd grown up in Queens and graduated from Brooklyn College. She moved to Harlem once she graduated. She's twenty-six years old. That number surprised me. I knew she was older than me, but I did not expect her to be four years older than me. She didn't judge me when she found out I didn't go to college. She respected my decision.

She was supposed to perform at 7:30pm. However, people didn't start flooding in until 7:45pm. The host hadn't showed up yet, and familiar faces to Silk were greeting her. Every person that infiltrated our conversation or gave Silk a hug, I glared into their eyes until they left. By the time 8pm reached, I was ready to go. I told Silk that I was heading out, but she shook her head.

"The host just sent a group text saying that he won't get here until 8:30. Ridiculous and unprofessional. Typical open-mic shit. I won't be performing here again or with that promoter."

"I don't blame you," I replied.

As I slid one arm into my jacket, I heard Silk say softly, "Lemme walk you to the bus or train."

I couldn't help but smile. "Okay, sure. Thanks."

There were no butterflies fluttering in my bashful belly. A simmering indescribable serenity soothed my stomach and I wanted Silk's presence to drape over my body like an evening gown.

As we walked towards the door, she made two leaps ahead of me and opened the door for me like the gentle-boi she is.

Our umbrella was the evening sky as we walked to the bus stop. The light rain felt nice as Silk spoke about a documentary she was working on. I wished to the winds under my breath that the bus would show up in twenty minutes. Sadly, my wish was ignored. As soon as we reached the bus stop, the B38 showed up swiftly in front of us.

She looked into my eyes. "Make sure you let me know when you get home so I know you're safe."

I nodded and wrapped my arms around her neck. I sneaked a whiff of her scent of frankincense. She slid her arms around my waist and squeezed. She didn't leave the bus stop until she saw me settled into a seat. She waved goodbye and smiled.

As the bus rode on, my body slowly surrendered to that simmering serenity that was soothing to my stomach.

I called up Annlea and Maggie to fill them in on the details.

Love With A Lil' Control

"Roxanne!" rang in my ears as I shot up out from my bed. My mother stripped the covers from body as I anticipated a smack to the face. I wasn't too sure what the issue was, but whenever Mama wakes me up at 3am in the morning, it's usually for something I didn't do right. However, I cleaned all the dishes and wiped down the sink. I swept all the floors and cleared the dining table off.

"So, you found out about that play from that Karla girl? Are you doing ungodly things with that girl, Roxanne?"

"No. It's 3 o'clock in the morning, Mama. This could've waited."

I slid the covers up from my ankles and turned my back to her and prepared to return to dreamland. Mama yanked the covers back off me and screamed, "Little girl, this is my house. I don't care what time it is in the morning. If I want answers from you, I'm gonna get them when I ask for them. You are so disrespectful. I pay all the bills."

"Mama, I'm not having sex with Karla. She told me about the play and I auditioned. It's called *Higher Heights*. That's it."

Mama looked into my eyes for a few seconds. Usually when she pulls this stunt, I cave in fear and feel bad. Not this time. I am getting tired of her random moments of shame dumping. She doesn't know about any of my past lady partners, and I wasn't about to start admitting it.

"Roxanne, I told you about being a part of things like this. It will only influence you even deeper to do more ungodly things."

I took a deep breath and replied, "Mama, for the umpteenth time, I de-converted from Christianity. That doesn't apply to me. There is nothing wrong with someone who loves the same sex. There is definitely nothing wrong with working with them and creating with people who are a part of the LGBTQ+ community."

Mama swung her back to me and whispered a prayer.

"I know one thing, you come home telling me about some woman you with, you better pack your things too. I've had enough of this mess. Me and my house, we gon' serve the lord. Yet, here you are. Gave your soul to the enemy and hanging around ungodly people."

I rolled my eyes, turned off the light, and wished my mother a goodnight.

I woke up the next morning to silence. The sun illuminated the bottom of my bed, and I couldn't help but smile at the yellow light. I was still feeling groggy from Mama's shenanigans last night, but seeing my friends today would liven me up. I rose to breathe in the silence and stretched. I walked over to the dining table to grab my phone. Mama placed a note on top of it that read:

Make sure you sweep the floor before you leave the house.

Miami And Change

I woke up four hours before my flight to make sure I had time for NYC traffic and for last minute details. The 3am air slipped into my sweater as I plopped my suitcase into the taxi's trunk. I didn't mind the coolness. I was ready to be refreshed. I already texted my mother, father, Annlea, and Maggie my itinerary. As the taxi rumbled over potholes and passed wee-hour junkies, I thought about the women from my past. All tucked away underneath my skin, waiting for their names to be called publicly as my love since I loved them in silence.

Too bad they'll remain underneath my skin. I can't stand the idea of being kicked out because Mama doesn't like the idea of her daughter with a woman. I don't have the space to be okay with losing friends and family, but I will make room for Silk. If she were to tell me she felt something deeply about me, my essence would declare her name to the streets. Mama would have to be okay that my heart is in the right hands; a woman's hands.

I dived into the last time Silk and I spoke on the phone. I let her know that I arrived home safely and thanked her for inviting me. I also filled her in on the shenanigans that happened on PicMyBiz between Johnson and me. She got really quiet after that. Maybe I shouldn't have told her, but I felt so comfortable to talk to her about my troubles. She hasn't reached out to me since. Granted that was only a few days ago, but I can't help but overthink.

The taxi pulled up to the airport, and I shook my neurotic thoughts away. The taxi driver pulled out my suitcase from the trunk. I paid him and walked straight to the front desk of my airline. Checking in with my airline, going through security check points and snagging breakfast only took forty-five minutes.

I sat at my gate at 6:15am munching on my bacon, lettuce, and tomato roll. I've never taken a plane with a first-class ticket, and I couldn't cease speculating what to expect. Would I receive vodka in a heart shaped glass? Would the flight attendant sing us covers from our favorite singers?

My flight was for 7:15am. I had an hour left, and I was contemplating whether or not I should call Silk. I didn't want to come off clingy, and I definitely didn't want her to think that I liked her. The last thing I need is for her to think I liked her and then get rejected. I chatted with Annlea for a bit until I was ready to board the plane.

Seat 3A was my seat, and seat 3B was vacant. It's going to be a good plane ride. I placed my headphones on and searched for my notebook in my backpack. I always loved to write while traveling. I pulled out my notebook and sat it in the seat next to me. I sat back and watched the various people in first class get settled. I assumed anyone who was in first class dressed as though they could afford to purchase seven extra seats if they wanted to.

Hot damn, I was wrong. People were draped in sweats, pajamas, suits, Sunday bests and *never-leaving-the-house* attire. I couldn't help but smile at to my own small-minded assumption. I slid my headphones down to wrap around my neck. I took a deep breath, sat back, and closed my eyes to listen to my present.

The laughing, bags opening, and seats reclining. Murmurs of beaches and nostalgic rendezvous. Crisp chips crumbling under excited teeth and glassed juices clanging against rings. I couldn't wait to go to Miami. I finally noticed my shoulders were up and my jaw was clenched. I released my jaw, then surrendered my shoulders to calmness.

∞

Upon checking in to the hotel, I watched my footsteps as I strolled over to the elevator to the third floor. The elevator's ding made me jolt once it reached my floor. I rushed over to my room and shut the door. I pressed my body to the door and sunk to the ground. So glad to be solo. I finally got up, threw my suitcase on the bed and unzipped it. I flipped open the top flap and rummaged around to find my bathing suit.

I pulled out my red and black two-piece swimwear and held it up in the air.

My hotel wasn't too far from the beach. I undressed, put on my bathing suit, and packed my beach bag. There was an amusement park, three museums, and two restaurants to visit during my time in Miami. I refused to be mentally consumed by a relationship that I was no longer in.

∞

The sun made me feel good as I strutted on the beach with my bag. I purchased a cheap beach chair from the boardwalk and found a spot farthest away from families. I wasn't in the mood for running children and screaming tantrums. Once I was settled, I took a few pictures of myself on my phone and posted one on PicMyBiz. I lost weight, yes, but I still looked good. I watched a few people eyeing me as I took my photos. Once I was done, I slowly slid back in my chair and gently caressed my left leg with my right foot. I closed my eyes and allowed my ears to take the lead. The waves made me feel as though my chest was open wide from its breeze and my heart felt light. The wind raced up my thighs and whisked past my torso softly. It felt good to be in this moment solo.

Elevator Passion

I purchased four outfits from Fifth and Alton, souvenirs for my loved ones, met a few people and ate some great food, including Twisted Cookin' and Dranks.

Shelly mentioned how delicious the food was, and Annlea told me her father had dined there as well.

I called a taxi to my hotel and paced the pavement while I waited. I texted Silk to wish her a good day and asked if we could talk. The taxi pulled up and I hopped in feeling upbeat.

"Hey, can you take me to the Wadding hotel, please?"

"Sure thing, beautiful. Where you from?"

I felt his eyeballs gawking at my breasts from his mirror. "New York, but if you don't mind, I got a lot on my mind right now and would like–"

"I got you, honey. This will be a quiet ride."

"Thanks."

My tummy rumbled as I imagined myself thirty years later with Johnson. I shook my head and thought of a man with no face in twenty years. I couldn't bear the thought. My mind trailed to Silk's smile. The ivory white gates and pink gums that spoke of ease and invitation. Her high cheekbones complimented every grin she's ever given me. I pictured us sitting on a roundabout porch in forty years. I shook out the weird thought of a lifetime commitment with a stranger. But…you know…

A breeze would tickle the bottom of my house dress as I rocked in my chair. Silk would be snapping greens on the porch steps while boasting about her youthful days as a filmmaker. My head hit the glass window that separated the taxi driver and me.

"Damn fool!" he yelled.

Nice way to return to the present.

"They get these fancy cars and act like they don't know what safe driving is. You okay, beautiful?"

"Yes, yes, I'm fine. Thanks for checking in."

"Sure thang."

He continued to drive, and I stayed with reality as I watched the various buildings of Miami. I watched the faces walking on the sidewalk that we passed, wondering what their stories were, hoping that one of them actually knew what it was like to suppress something that was fundamental to who they were.

As soon as I recognized the flagpole that was three blocks away from the hotel, I dug into my purse to grab a twenty-dollar bill. I slipped it out and sat back into my seat until he pulled up.

"Aight, beautiful, we're here. You have a good day."

"Thanks for the ride."

I handed him the twenty dollars. "Keep the change, sir."

I scooched out of the taxi and watched him drive away.

Once I reached to the hotel lobby, the woman at the front desk waved me over, "Ms. Patterson."

I walked over to the desk and eyeballed the note in her hand. "Hey, what's going on?"

"Well, Ms. Patterson, you have a message. Your mother called."

She handed me the note and I nodded.

"Thanks. My mother is so old school. She knows I have a phone"

We both giggled.

I rushed over to the elevator and waited for the doors to open. I heard footsteps behind me and a tap on the shoulders, "Hey, did you press the button up, honey?"

When I looked over my shoulder, my eyes were met with a walking canvas made by every god humankind has ever invented.

Thick calves, wide hips and a waist that looked good to kiss. She had a body I'd love to slide my tongue on. Her dark brown shoulders shimmered under the lights while the rest of her dress draped her body like sheer curtains at an island resort. I was in a momentary bliss.

"Well, you're not much of a talka I see."

She glanced at the lit-up elevator button, sized me up and smiled.

"So, that's why you ain't speakin'. Too busy lookin' like you wanna fuck me. Ain't that right, honey?"

Watching her lips move made my knees feel rubbery. Her candor made my chest stiffen.

"You're beautiful, yes. But I don't fuck strangers. I like your dress."

She winked at me and walked into the elevator. I watched as her booty swayed into the metal box. She looked at me and cocked her head to the side. Her box braids fell softly to the side with her.

"Goin' up...or goin' down?"

"Oh, yes of course. I was just making sure everybody was all in."

What the hell? Who says that? Damn. Now she thinks I'm vapid.

I quickly looked down at myself and realized how good I looked in my bikini top and denim shorts. With her hand in the door, I noticed her eyes lingering on my shorts. I smiled and glided inside the elevator. Her hand abandoned the door, and I watched the doors kiss shut. No music played, and I'm sure neither of us gave a damn. As much as I wanted to run from such direct magnetism that cackled and sparked between us, I surrendered to it.

"What are you doing in Miami?"

"Conference. I am a software engineer, and I wanna meet some new folk out here that do what I do. I'm from Ohio. You? I see you went to the beach."

I made sure to look into her eyes, and I slowly inhaled. I smelled a vintage version of the cologne, Escapade and beamed. I slid my tongue out slowly. With my hand slowly gliding down my breast, torso and pelvis, I replied, "Yeah. I got some sun, waves, and few pictures. I'm here on vacation."

Her nipples began to peak through her dress, and she quickly crossed her arms.

"Cold?" I asked.

She nodded and took a step forward. I took a step forward. The elevator slightly rumbled, and the doors opened. She stroked my arm with one of her moisturized fingers and whispered in my ear, "Wanna come to my room?"

I tapped my pocket that had the note of my mother's message, and I looked down at the elevator carpet. Her scent was inviting. I took a step towards the door, and she squealed.

"Good. This is going to be fun. Haven't had none since my last trip out here three months ago. Bring your fine ass here into this room."

The thought of me and this woman texting after a sinful and lusty encounter made my heart race. I don't have the energy to hide another woman. As she skipped out the elevator, I remained inside and let the door close.

"Tease," she yelled out.

I let one of the elevator walls hold my body as I exhaled relief. I would like to live under a roof. She ain't worth losing housing.

The elevator rumbled, and I ran out the elevator. I sped to my room and slipped inside. I dropped my beach bag on the bed and looked out window. There are beautiful women out there that love women. There are beautiful women out there that are attracted to me. I shook my head and called my mother up.

"Hey Mama, how you doin'?"

"Hey yourself, I called you twice yesterday. Where were you? Are you okay? You better be behaving out there. What outfits did you pack? I did not see any of your outfits. I hope you didn't pack that two-piece bathing suit."

"I sure did pack that bathing suit. I look good in it. I packed all the outfits I liked. I'm okay. I have a few more hours left of this vacation, and I'd like to enjoy it without you fussin' at me, Mama."

"Don't get all high and rude now that you're away on vacation. You still live under my roof, and I'm still your Mama. And I told you about wearing that bathing suit, Roxanne. It's immodest and sends the wrong message. I'm glad you're okay. What did you do?"

Irritation engulfed my lungs and I wanted to scream.

"I'll tell you when I get home, Mama."

"Is Johnson there with you? Is that why you're rushing me off the phone?"

"No, Mother," I replied through my teeth.

"Watch your tone, gal. I asked you a question. I am your mother."

"I'm rushing you off the phone so I can enjoy what's left of my vacation."

She was silent.

"Hello? Mama, you there?"

"Bye, Roxanne."

Without my response she ended the call. Was I wrong? She was being irritating and asking the wrong things. She's still fussing with me about outfits, behaving and some abusive ex. I breathed in the hotel smell and released our phone conversation. I packed up my things while texting Annlea and Maggie about the beautiful woman I met by the elevator. They felt like I should have gone to her room, but it just didn't feel right. Having my mother call me repeatedly while potentially being between the legs of an immaculate woman, would definitely screw everything up. As I peeled off my bathing suit and got ready to go in the shower, three bangs at the door made me shudder. Did Johnson find me? *Fuck, where is my pepper spray.* I ran to my bag as two more bangs shook my hotel door. My hands played hide and seek until I retrieved my pepper spray.

"Roxanne," screamed through the door.

I tiptoed to the door and peered through the peephole. It was a man, and he was waving my identification card in the peephole. I noticed he was in the hotel's uniform and nodded.

I opened the door about an inch so he wouldn't see my naked body and eyed my ID. I snatched it out of his hand, thanked him, and closed my door. I took a deep breath and felt like a magnet to the floor as my body slid down to the carpet. Hot tears fell and it wouldn't stop. I breathed in deep, and my throat cried out.

I surrendered. The tears, the whimpers, the lamenting, the tarrying. I let it flow. As my heart paced at a slower rate, I remembered Dr. Ramsey's note. I struggled to rise from the floor and dragged my body to my bag. I zipped open the pouch on the side and stared at the folded piece of paper. *Lastly, the abuse is not your fault* carouselled throughout my mind as I pulled out the note and read it aloud:

Roxy, please remember these six important things
- If you return to him, it's okay to seek help.
- The desire to hide what really happened in your relationship with Johnson is okay, but counterproductive towards healing and moving forward.
- Feeling guilt and shame about what he did to you is normal, but it isn't justified.
- Lastly, the abuse is not your fault.

When you're ready, call anytime to make an appointment!

-Dr. Ramsey.

I think it's about time I make this appointment.

Hot Water

Thank goodness it was finally getting warmer. April had gotten off to a great start by giving us leather jacket weather. I was beginning to see speckles of color splashed along the trees. It was warm enough for me to walk around the park across the street from my job in the mornings. I'd get off the bus a stop earlier and walked through Prospect Park to reach my job. I adored being coated by trees, greenery, and morning chirps of blue jays. I let my thoughts settle in with soft steps and sporadic jogger breaths.

Today was the last day that my co-workers and bosses would see my face until next Monday. I'd taken tomorrow and Friday off because the musical was tomorrow. I watched a squirrel cross my path and tumble into the grass. I was ecstatic about this musical, and now I'd rather curl up in a ball.

A year ago, I would've felt more grounded than a clean 92nd street sidewalk. I hadn't performed at an open mic in ages, and I didn't plan on going to any for a while.

Every time Johnson and I attended an event, he'd embarrass me. Either he was heckling, laughing loudly for people to look at him, or he would start arguments with people. Whenever he found out I was going to an event, he invited himself. I made sure to tell him nothing about the musical. Next thing you know, he'll start an argument with an audience member or even worse: jump on the stage and make himself a part of the musical.

It always felt like some competition with that guy.

Looking down at my hands, both were in fists. I breathed into the present and released the anger I felt about Johnson's past shenanigans. I invited my Mama and Daddy to come. My Daddy accepted and Mama refused to attend. She scrunched up her nose and shook her head.

"I don't wanna' see no mess like that. A musical that approves of that abomination? No, thank you."

Meanwhile, her daughter just might be a part of that group. I wonder how she would feel if she found out she birthed an abomination.

A rush of wind pulled me back to the park and out of the depths of my mind. I wanted to text Silk. I wanted to see to her again. I craved to smell her scent of frankincense, sweat, grit, and honey. But I knew better.

I walked out of the park and crossed the street. Before I walked inside the library, I saw two old ladies holding hands and laughing as they walked out. They looked as though they found safety and a home within the crevices of the others' smiles. They had joy. They had love and I witnessed all of it within the four seconds I watched them. I rushed inside.

As I was unzipping my jacket on the escalator, I heard kisses and saw Shelly at the top of the escalator with all her teeth exposed.

"Hey, girl."

I waved and was met with her arm looped in mine when I reached the top of the escalator.

"Tomorrow is the day you get to sing your heart out on stage. You excited? The boss bought doughnuts in to wish you good luck."

I looked ahead and smiled as we walked toward the office door.

"Yeah, I'm excited. I haven't sung in front of an audience in a while."

She released my arm and opened the door for me. "Is Johnson going to meet you there or is he going to pick you up?"

"He's going to pick me up," I lied.

She followed me quietly to my cubicle. As I placed my jacket over the chair, I anticipated the muffled sound of her heels clomping down the carpeted row of cubicles. I plopped in my chair and finally breathed. I felt her still standing over my cubicle. I spun my chair to the left, leaned on the arm rest and waited.

She tilted her head and finally replied, "You sure?"

"About what?"

"About Johnson picking you up. Are you sure?"

I couldn't help but frown. *Why does she care?*

"Yeah, I'm sure. Why so concerned? You still going right, Shelly?"

"Sorry, Roxy. My man is finally in town and I can't let that pass by. You know we have a long-distance relationship. I gotta get this dick when I can, girl." She chuckled to herself.

I wriggled my mouth around to gift her an understandable smile, but all I could give was no more enthusiastic than a child going to the dentist.

"I feel you, girl."

I turned on my computer and concentrated my eyes on the start-up screen, hoping she would get a hint and leave.

She leaned forward and whispered, "You sure you and Johnson are back together? You've been so quiet about stuff lately. He hasn't been around and you've never mentioned anything about him coming. You spoke about the musical, what it's about, your role, your Daddy coming, but you never mentioned anything about Johnson."

She's on to me. I've never been a good liar, but I at least thought that she would've simply believed that he was going to pick me up.

"Why is it so important to you? Why are you so fixated on whether my man is coming or not?"

Shelly stood straight up and placed her arms in the air. "Damn, girl. I surrender. I was just concerned about you is all."

She waved me off and walked away to her cubicle. My stomach felt as though it froze in place as I watched her walk away.

Whatever. I will be away from this place for four days.

I walked over to the bite-sized lunchroom and observed my co-workers munching away at the doughnuts and cold hot cocoa that came in a box. I smiled, thanked, nodded, and pretended the small talk amused my heart. They couldn't give a rat's ass if I was a part of a musical or not. They were there for the doughnuts and another reason to gossip. I understood.

∞

Backstage, my face felt warm, and my heart was on fire. A make-up artist did all of our faces, and it was wonderful. I don't put make-up on much, so seeing my eyebrows thick and lips a salacious red looked phenomenal. Once the show began, clothes were ricocheting around the dressing room. With only one song to perform, I helped the other actors get dressed and helped others clean up their allotted areas.

By this time, we all got along, and we were all ready to light up the stage in our own ways. Silk's part didn't involve singing at all. She had a leading role of a heartbreaker who never really knew who she was until she meets someone that forces her character to re-discover herself.

She whizzed from backstage to the stage within moments and, man, was it a sight to see. Every time she slid into the dressing room, my eyes followed her hands unbuttoning and unzipping her pants. She'd wiggle her hips a few times to slide her pants off, revealing her black boxer briefs. Her thick thighs and hearty breasts looked delicious. I couldn't help but wonder what my taste buds would discover if my tongue initialed her name on her inner thighs.

"Roxy, can you pass me the green overalls behind you, please?"

"Oh, sure."

I ripped the overalls off the hanger and tossed it at her.

"Thanks."

"Uh huh," I replied.

Silk smirked as she stepped into the pants of the overalls and pulled them past her deep brown thighs. She looked up at me and grinned, almost losing her balance as she fought to tug the overalls past her butt. I dove towards her so she wouldn't fall. I looked at the ground and counted to five.

I felt her watching me. I eventually watched her feet scurry around as she searched for boots, and I wished upon the stage lights that I'd disappear. Once she ran out of the dressing room, I walked to the left side of the backstage exit and peeked through the door. Almost every seat in the theatre was filled. I spotted my father and smiled until I also spotted Karla, my ex-girlfriend.

I know she told me about this musical, but I didn't even consider the fact that she would attend. I peeped her cleavage and maroon spaghetti straps. She must be wearing that dress she wore on our first date. I remember.

She smelled like coconut oil, honey suckle and strawberry lemonade that evening. With each step we took together down the Brooklyn blocks to Juniors Restaurant, I couldn't help but sneak a few sniffs of her. Her black coils bounced with us and danced to the rhythm of her high heel boots. I loved to make her laugh just to see her cock her head back. Her laughter made her teeth a spotlight for the moment.

My phone vibrated and I closed the backstage exit door. I pulled my phone out of my blue blazer and saw Johnson's name pop up.

Just bought a ticket to your lil' play. Let's see how good it will be.

My body was vibrating. I felt like my throat was shimmying down to my stomach. I couldn't have this guy make a damn scene because he wants all the attention. What if he makes a loud homophobic outburst? What if he randomly starts strumming his guitar like he did at my audition at the Dynasty Theater audition?

Tony's quick jog towards my direction lured me back into the present.

"Hey, Roxanne, you're up in like ten minutes. You ready?"

I looked down at my outfit and smiled.

"Yep. I just need to take off my blazer. Thanks for the heads up, Tony."

We both sped towards the dressing room and I danced out of my blazer. Silk was still on stage and I couldn't help but feel giddy at the thought that we would share the stage for a few moments. I focused on my breathing as I prepared myself to get on stage.

I inhaled for five seconds, held it for five seconds, and exhaled for five seconds. I did it three more times until everything within me felt calm. I waited behind the curtain for my cue to hit the stage. I heard the magic line and paced slowly towards the limelight as I began to sing. Heart racing but feeling as though it would leap out of my chest, I felt like a phoenix rising out of the ashes. I looked at Silk and felt at ease. When I finished my number, I fell into the background as the next scene went on.

Johnson still hadn't arrived, and I was grateful. I spoke with the others backstage about singing and future projects. The idea of showcasing my music to an intimate audience began to brew in my belly, and I was getting full. As I cackled, sipped wine and cheese with the other performers, I felt excited for the remainder of the year. Once the show was over, I walked over to my father, who was beaming.

"Darling, you did a great job. I'm so glad to see you singing again. What a nice musical, too."

"Thanks, Pops. Yeah, it has a good storyline."

"Yes, it does. Listen, your little boyfriend is here."

"Yeah, he told me he would come. Did he talk to you? Where is he?"

My father sucked his teeth and shook his head. "Yeah, he went to the concession stand in the back to get an energy drink. He's insufferable, and I must tell you for the fiftieth time, there's something about him that isn't right, darling."

I saw the bouquet of roses in my father's hand and looked down at the row of seats.

I felt his finger lift my head up. "Roxanne, what's wrong?"

He handed me the roses and kissed my forehead.

"We broke up. We're not even together. I didn't invite him. But he has a right to buy a ticket to a public event."

"I'm sorry, excuse me. Hello, you must be Roxanne's dad," Jan said, reaching out to shake his hand as he met her halfway.

"Yes, and you're Jan, right?"

"Yes, your daughter did great tonight. She's got a lovely voice. Does it run in the family?"

My father chuckled. "Absolutely not. I sing with the grace of eight cats in heat, but I try to bring it down to five kittens."

As we all laughed, Johnson walked up to us. With his eyebrows furrowed and his jaw clenched he said, "You're wearing make-up."

"Yes, she looks good with it. You are beautiful without it too," Jan replied.

My father looked into Johnson's eyes.

"Yes, she looks great."

"Thanks a lot." I smiled.

Johnson took a step back. As Jan and my father conversed the theme of the musical and the story behind it, Johnson looked at me in disgust. Someone tapped my shoulder. I turned and it was Silk.

"Hey! You did great, Silk. Phenomenal acting!"

She flashed a smile and hugged me. "Thanks, Queen."

I interrupted Jan and my father, "Hey Daddy, this is Silk. Silk, this is my father, Mr. Patterson."

She shook his hand and smiled. "Nice to meet you, Mr. Patterson."

As the four us spoke about the musical, Johnson observed with a scowl on his face. Jan attempted to draw him in.

"So, I know you came a little late, but from what you saw, how was it for you?"

Johnson shrugged. "It was okay. I honestly feel as though this musical had an agenda to accept people of an alternative lifestyle that I just can't get down with, you know? I mean no offense to you, Jan, or Satin."

"It's Silk, boy. My name is Silk," Silk retorted.

Johnson snorted. "Okay, Silk, my bad. Anyway, I just feel like, nowadays y'all just want to throw that stuff in our face. It's too much."

A familiar voice behind him boomed, "Well, that means you must not really like your own girl, then." Karla's face appeared, just over Johnson's shoulder.

A familiar voice, standing behind him boomed.

"Karla. Hey, girl," I nervously said, then gestured to Johnson and Karla

"He's my ex who attended, uninvited."

"Silk and Jan, this is Karla, my ex. And Silk and Jan, this is Karla, my (other) ex."

"A lot of exes poppin' up on you huh, Roxanne?" Jan teased.

We all laughed as I shook my head.

My father smiled and embraced Karla. "Ah, yes. I remember you. How's your mother?"

"She's doing well, Mr. Antoine. Still looking young out here, I see."

"Yeah. It runs in the family."

Johnson's gaze was still on me. He gripped his energy drink tightly, and I'm sure he was pretending it was my neck.

Karla shook her head and wished us all goodnight.

Johnson picked up his guitar and walked away.

My father looked into my eyes until I spoke up.

"I'm currently seeing a counselor. Her name is Dr. Ramsey. She's cool. I've been to a few sessions and it's helping me really see how much I need to value myself and how bad he is for me."

"Roxanne."

I wouldn't let him finish. The water was beginning to rise in my eyeballs, and I couldn't break down in that theatre.

"Pops, I can't do this right now. Please."

"Okay, darling. I want you to remember that you are not alone and that I will always love you. You are accepted and loved by your father. Don't you forget that."

I wrapped my arms around him as I allowed his black sweater to mask my face. As his sweater soaked up my tears, he embraced me tightly. I nuzzled my face into him and looked up at him.

"I gotta go, Pops. Thanks for coming."

I walked to the stage, pushed the backstage door open and scanned the room. I spotted my blue canvas bag and leather jacket sitting next to someone's stage costume on a rack. I snagged my things, walked back to where my father was and squeezed his hand. I swung my coat around my shoulders and walked out of the theatre.

The brisk evening enveloped me and refreshed what little of my skin that was exposed to it. I walked down eighth avenue, listening to my heels and the laughter of a couple passing by. With Johnson not following me, I felt a little at ease within myself. Reaching Seventh avenue, the medley of lights paralleled what was going on in the inside of me.

Chianne's BBQ's sign caught my eye, and my stomach nudged me across the street.

Quickly scanning the faces that passed me by, I felt high. Strutting with my back straight and my hips switching, I thought about my song book in my bag.

I pushed the door into the restaurant and walked right up to the beaming server.

"Well, hello, Ma'am. Welcome to Chianne's BBQ. Whoa, you are glowing, woman!"

"Thanks," I replied with a smile plastered on my face.

"Table for two?" she asked.

Before I could release the first syllable, I jolted to Johnson's voice.

"Yes, thanks."

I spun around immediately feeling my chest vibrate. He placed his hands on my hips, twisted them forward and whispered, "Move. Walk. Let's go."

The server was already walking forward. I moved forward as if anchors were hooked over my ankles, trying to drag me to some sort of defeat I couldn't name. As we sat down and looked over the menu, Johnson sporadically huffed and puffed. I was waiting for him to blow a pig's house down and maybe pass out from all that unnecessary mouth breathing.

As he shot death glares at me, my leg jittered up and down. In anticipation of an irrational outburst, my stomach tightened. Appetite? What appetite?

I ordered a warm water and a salad. He ordered ribs, fries, and a soda. When the server walked away, he finally spoke up.

"What's with all that damn make-up on your face? The show is over. Take it off. You're beautiful without all that shit on your face."

"No," I snapped back. "I like it and I'm keeping it on until I get home."

He looked away and allowed the surrounding chatter to fill the space between us.

"And why did you invite that woman to your show? You tryna embarrass me?" He raised his voice with each syllable.

Something within me broke and something else turned on. "First of all, Karla is the one who told me about the musical. Second, lower your damn voice. Just say you ain't like the play. Also, we're not together, fool. I don't have to answer to you."

Gradually I relaxed; my leg stopped its frantic up-and-down motion. Glimmerings of hunger fluttered in my stomach.

He smirked a little and shook his head. "You know, Roxy, you're just making this news easier for me."

"What news?"

"I like someone. She loves me. So, if you wanna make this work, you'd better speak up now or lose me forever."

Seeing Dr. Ramsey had really helped for sure. Now I could really see through all his bullshit. She told me to really listen to his words without twisting or turning what my morals and gut have chosen for me, no matter what.

I smiled at him. "We're not together. Go be with her."

He heaved and punched his cushioned booth seat. "Roxy, you're clearly missing the point here."

I couldn't help but chuckle for a few moments.

"Roxy, I'm glad you think your overbearing ways are funny, but this is no laughing matter. We are at a bad place in our relationship."

"We're not in a relationship, Johnson!" I yelled.

Our food arrived and we ate in silence as I reflected on the buffoon who sat in front of me.

I heard Dr. Ramsey's voice from one of our sessions in my head.

"If you leave, you will be able to live without him. Relationships require respect on both sides, love on both sides and passion. Do you have those things with him? Are you happy with him? This is our eighth session and you've mentioned past exes who were women...whether you stay or go, remember: Your passions, dreams, family and happiness are important."

Never one to sugarcoat with me, Dr. Ramsey was finally making sense. *I am worthy and my needs are important too.*

Once I finished my salad, I said his name and looked into his eyes.

"Stop trying to reel me back in. It's over. You just said that you like another woman and that she loves you already. Go be with her."

He was quiet. He stopped eating, and a few tears began to run down his face.

"Roxy, I'm just trying to love you the best way I can. In order to do that, I need to check my limits. Why won't you just let me love you? All you do is run your mouth, back talk and argue with me. Then you make yourself a part of some musical that makes me look bad to my family. You are something else. All I'm saying is that there are other women out there ready to be with me."

There was so much I wanted to say, so much I wanted to do, but I knew better. Dr. Ramsey told me to not search for patterns but pay attention when patterns show themselves to me and, damn it, these were some patterns. I couldn't believe I was just now catching onto his tactics.

"Look, I told you that I am not going to be with you. Throwing another woman in my face ain't gonna work."

His tears were now dried up, and he looked into my eyes. He continued to eat his food and eventually shrugged.

"Well, I'm mad at you still, Roxy. It's not always about you. It's like I'm talking to a brick wall."

I returned the shrug and added a smirk. "Well, then, leave this wall alone and go find someone who is open to what you want instead of trying to break down this wall."

He shook his head. "What else do you want from me?"

This guy.

"Nothing."

"Okay. You want to be selfish and deny my concerns, then fine, Roxy. Oh, and by the way, it's one of my co-workers who is in love with me. She'd do anything for me. Including the things, you're too good to do. We've been dating since you broke up with me. You know, since we're over and all."

"Fine, Johnson. Have fun."

I grabbed my jacket, slid out of my booth seat, and walked towards the door.

"That's not how we do things, Roxanne. Get back here."

I fed him silence as I walked out of the restaurant.

I hailed a taxi to take me home.

Later on, that night, I called Annlea and Maggie. I filled them in about the show, seeing Karla and Johnson showing up.

Before I hung up Maggie asked, "You keep mentioning this Silk girl. What's the deal? You gonna tell her how you feel now that you and Johnson are over with?"

With a smile so big my jaw ached I replied, "Oh, no. I know she doesn't feel the same. I'll keep seeing my counselor and loving life. I don't have time to deal with anybody."

We said our goodnights and hung up. I took a shower and got ready for bed. My phone vibrated.

It was Johnson. I took a deep breath and ignored his call.

The next morning, I texted Silk to ask how she was doing. She invited me to a show her friend was doing on April 24th. I asked for details. She mentioned that her friend, Gia, just released a mixtape and will be performing a few of her songs in Greenpoint, Brooklyn. Nervous and excited, I texted back yes.

The First Session

Four days after the musical, I was scheduled to see Dr. Ramsey. As soon as I melted into the couch, she sat up straight and flashed me a smile. "Whoa, someone dropped some dead weight. You are glowing, Roxy. How have you been since we last spoke?"

My heart couldn't help but flutter after her inference of my body language and appearance.

"Well…The musical went great."

"How did you feel after the musical was over?"

"I felt good. Accomplished. All of a sudden, I had so many ideas for new music. I think I'm ready to perform more frequently now."

"Why didn't you feel as though you weren't ready before?"

"I was, but after a while, Johnson's negative comments, lack of encouragement and self-centered outburst made me feel like I should stop."

"How so, Roxy?"

I hate when she wanted more.

"Well, when I was with him, every time I did a show, he'd be obnoxious just to bring the attention to himself or try to take advantage. So, I either do the show without him knowing or don't perform at all. But not anymore. I don't care anymore. I have a gift to share so I'm gonna share it. I created two new songs, hung out with my friends, spoke with my father for four hours on the phone, and I even bought some new outfits to wear. There is this yellow romper that I purchased at the boutique down the block from here and it's wonderful. Silk and I have been texting each other every day too and— "

Dr. Ramsey waved her hand in the air for me to stop talking.

"Whoa," she chuckled. "That's a lot of improvement and good news. But who is Silk? That's a new name."

My leg became a piston. I took a deep breath and spoke quicker than an auctioneer. "Well, I met her during the first day of my audition for the play in February. She's amazing. She has these big beautiful brown eyes, thick hips, a chill personality, and she wrote and directed an award-winning documentary. It feels like I've known her all my life—or at least I've met her in my past life or something; I don't know. All I know is, she had my attention since I first met her, but it's, like, what I am gonna do? I don't know if she likes me."

Dr. Ramsey blinked a few times in my direction.

"Dr. Ramsey?"

She exhaled and tilted her head to the side. "Where do you see yourself for the rest of the year? What would you like to achieve in your life?"

I haven't written a list of goals in almost a year and a half. My mind felt as though a list of words were being dumped into my brain. There was so much that I wanted to do. This musical had opened my eyes to so many possibilities.

"I know I sprung that question up on you, but it's not for you to answer now. When you get home and settled, reflect on it. Write down five things you want to see in your life by the end of the year. Read them to yourself and then on a separate piece of paper write down ten things you are willing to release in order to achieve the things on the first paper."

Dr. Ramsey scribbled on some paper without looking up. I waited a few moments for her look up at me. Whatever she was writing, it was beginning to feel like a paragraph so I spoke up.

"Release? What do you mean?"

"Well, you want to move out of your mother's home. What would you have to release in order to do so? Would it be to release bad spending habits to save more, or release a low paying job and get a better paying one. You get me?"

I nodded fast and breathed in deeply. I couldn't wait to get home. I'll take a nice bath, wash my hair, mask my face, clean my section of the apartment and write these lists. We spoke about worth and how our life belongs to no one other than ourselves. We owe it to ourselves to treat our bodies, mind and emotions right. When the session was over, I decided to walk over to Serene's Coffee shop.

I saw the metal gates closed down and the lights off. It was only 3pm. Serene's Coffee Shop closed at 7pm on weekdays. I looked around for a sign and found nothing. There was another person pacing on the other side of the store. Maybe there was a sign on that side. I walked over to the corner and spotted Karla frowning at the metal gates.

"No snacks for us, I guess," I said, startling her.

"Oh, hey there, Roxy. Yeah, I guess so. Do you know what happened? I was just here last week. Nothing was said."

"Nope, I'm just as lost on this as you are."

Karla looked down further and saw a sign on the ground. She marched over, picked it up, faced me and read it aloud, "After thirty years of being a part of this community, Serene's Coffee Shop is permanently closed. Thanks for your business."

I shook my head and replied, "How much do you wanna bet it's probably gonna be replaced by some chain coffee shop?"

"Of course. That's always the case. Anyway, I'll just head home. It was nice to see you. Great job last week. Wonderful voice you have."

She walked up to me and slowly whispered in my ear. Her breath tickling in my ear made my spine wanna whine slowly for her entertainment.

"I'll call you later, Roxanne."

I backed up and nodded, "Yeah, sure, Karla. Later."

I spun around and walked towards the B38 bus.

∞

After submerging myself in hot water, Epson salt and lavender, I felt tranquil. Mama was in her bedroom on the phone with her best friend, so I knew I had some alone time for a while. At least three hours. With two fingers from each hand, I applied the black charcoal mud mask in circular motions. As I looked in the mirror, I called myself a plethora of things: *Beautiful, Kind, Talented, Compassionate, Driven, Determined, Smart, Soulful, Beautiful Voice*. Each word made me smile, and I made sure to repeat each one at least three times. As the mask was drying, I put on my pajamas and sat at the living room table. I grabbed a pen and ripped out two pages from my legal memo pad.

I closed my eyes and gave all my attention to my breathing. Accepted my mother's voice cackling in her room, the man walking outside our window blasting his music, heavy footsteps from our neighbor upstairs. I breathed in the present moment and exhaled any thoughts that riled up any negative emotions. After about ten minutes, I opened my eyes and began to write:

My top 5 Goals for 2015
➢ Be more confident accepting of myself: ALL OF ME.
➢ Release my ep.
➢ Work on a plan to move out
➢ Tell my Mama my truth.
➢ Be in a healthy, blissful and evolving relationship

I read the list aloud and felt my shoulders stiffen. I folded the paper in half and placed it gently in my lap. I lightly slammed my hand on the top of the second paper and slid it in front of me. I watched my fingers tap the page as I thought of what to write. As my fingers stopped tapping, I let silence take over.

I scribbled:

-A higher paying job by the end of summer
-Work on songwriting every day
-Save money by not eating out, going out, or drinking
-Whatever it takes to achieve them all.

I texted my father, Annlea, Maggie, and Silk goodnight. They all responded back, but Silk's response made me smile.

Sleep well, Roxy. I hope you wake up refreshed.

I heard my mother shout from her bedroom, "Them dishes better be washed, Roxanne. I'll wake you right up if I see any dishes in that sink."

"Okay, Mama."

I cleaned the dishes that I didn't dirty in the sink and went to bed. Hopefully, I'll be outta this house soon.

Bbq's And Lost Magic

Annlea, Maggie, and I went out to eat at Bubba BBQ's downtown Manhattan. It's been a while since we all were able to hang out. I needed it. The laughs, the smirks, the hugs, tears… I needed all of it. The loud chattering, wild cackles from us and the tables around us felt refreshing.

Our jumbo-sized drinks kept us company as we waited for our entrées.

"So, wait a damn minute, this man shows up to the play to tell you that he's dating somebody else? What for?" Maggie giggled.

"Yep. To make me jealous and come crawling back to him," I replied.

"He's probably fucking that co-worker," Annlea chimed in.

Nodding in agreement, I took a long sip of my long island iced tea. I smiled and replied, "A part of me feels like it was his last attempt to control me."

Annlea and Maggie looked at each other and shook their heads.

"It's all good though. My eyes are set on Silk. If I found out that she feels the same, it's on."

Maggie struggled to finally speak past the laughter, "Damn, girl. You barely know her. You think she's your person?"

My face quieted their laughter, and I shifted in my seat. "Yes, I do. There's something about her that feels as though I've met her before. She feels like home. She's intriguing. She's smart, funny, witty, fine, and has a heart of gold. Whenever we text, I get nervous, yes, but I also feel as though I am communicating with a longtime friend who I'd like to have sex with."

Annlea placed her hand onto of mine. "Roxy, I don't know who Silk is. I have yet to meet her, but she obviously left a swooned impression on you. If you really feel that way, then you need to tell your mother. What if Silk actually does feel the same? Your ass will be in a sticky situation 'cause a love like that, you won't be able to keep a secret."

As I began to grin and had a little hope of Silk being my partner, Maggie's stern face let me know she was about to throw some realistic jargon my way.

She shook her head and pointed her finger in my direction. "Nah, you going too far out. First of all, you still need to get to know her. Then you need to get your heart ready for rejection or acceptance. You never know. She might have a chick on the low. Maybe she's straight, maybe you're not her type. Maybe she does feel the same. If so, then still. No need to be telling your mommy for a while. You need to make sure she worth being surely thrown out of your house. I think you should tell your mother once you move out of the house."

I wanted to curse her out and storm off. She had a point, *I know.*

I just sighed and sipped my drink and watched our server walk down the aisle towards us with two food trays in her hand.

She placed both trays on our table and slid our plates in front us. We all thanked her, and I watched her bubble butt switch from side to side as she walked away.

As our hands fluttered around our food, Maggie spoke up, "So, when are you going to see Silk again, anyway."

I perked up and said, "April 24th."

"Okay, girl. No need to announce it," Annlea chuckled.

"She invited me to her friend's show. Her friend is singing songs from her most recent mixtape."

We ate in silence for a few moments until Annlea nudged me and winked. "So, Maggie. How you and Grandpa doing?"

Maggie was about to pop a french fry in her mouth, but flung it in Annlea's direction. As it smacked the middle of Annlea's head, we all cackled.

Annlea shrugged, ate the fry and said, "Well, how you are you and Grandpa Tedrick?"

"He's only nine years older than me. My goodness. Anyway, we're doing good. He invited me to join him to New Orleans this weekend. He just got a promotion and wants to celebrate with me on his arm. I'm excited for good food and vacation dick."

We all cackled. "Vacation what, Maggie?" I asked.

"Ya'll heard me. Vacation dick hits different. It's stress-free so it has more energy to take care of my needs."

We laughed until our faces were red. Annlea told us how much she appreciated being single and Maggie went on about how she cooked for Tedrick for the first time, and he made love to her in the kitchen in response.

"Ain't nothin' betta than good sex after stew oxtails."

I smirked and nodded knowing damn well I couldn't relate.

"I'll be right back ya'll. I gotta pee."

I rushed to the bathroom, whipped out my phone from my vest pocket and checked my phone for any texts from Silk.

Hey, Ms. Roxanne. This is a BYOB event. Can you bring a bottle of Rosé?

I texted her back that I would and hurried back to the table.

"I've never seen anyone so jolly after peeing. Who you saw in there?" Annlea asked.

"Oh, please. She probably ain't even use the bathroom," Maggie chimed in.

"I was texin' back Silk. She asked me to bring some Rosé since it's a BYOB event we're going to."

They both looked at each other and looked at their almost empty plates.

"What?" I asked.

They both grinned.

April 24th

    I dropped my keys on the living room table and rushed out of my work clothes. I jogged to the bathroom and turned the shower on. I looked into the mirror and stared at myself for a while. I had my Daddy's dark brown eyes and my mother's high cheekbones. Steam slowly began to cover my reflection, and I watched the fog blanket my eyes, noses, lips, and chin. I slid my hand across the mirror and smiled at the wet reflection.

    I waited patiently to arrive back home to prepare for my night out with Silk. When I wrote April 24th on documents earlier at work, Silk's face would pop up in my mind. I stepped into the shower and let the water wash away the day's work, sweat and city commute. I kept seeing repeating numbers throughout the day. Every time I looked at the time, it was a sequence of: 11:11am, 1:11pm, 2:22pm and 4:44pm. I ordered a bagel with strawberry cream cheese, hot chocolate, and a banana. The total came up to $7.77. I think all the repeating numbers are some kind of sign that I'm doing the right thing or that I'm on the right path. Yet, I still felt nervous. My outfit, hair, perfume, and personality had to be perfect for Silk. When I got out of the shower, I used an oil that I'd purchased from a vendor on Flatbush Avenue. It smelled like lavender and honey. I dabbed some on my neck, behind my ears, and on my wrists. I planned my outfit ahead of time. I bought that yellow dress at the boutique downtown just for this occasion. I dried off, moisturized, and checked my phone. Annlea and Maggie, both texted me in our group message. They assured me that being myself was enough. I took pictures of myself in my outfit and sent it to them in the group message. They loved my twist out hairdo and how the yellow complimented my complexion. My best friends approved the yellow romper and big gold hoop earrings. Therefore, it's the best outfit. Those are the rules.

Silk and I planned to meet up at 6:45pm at the train station. From there, we would walk to the venue together. What would we talk about? I gotta find topics to talk about.

I stepped into my yellow dress, pulled it up and ran back to the bathroom to look in the mirror. My friends were right, my twist out looked great. I grabbed the can of olive oil sheen that was on the bathroom windowsill and sprayed my hair for three seconds. I loved when my hair shimmered. Curly, shiny kinks, combined with a knockout romper that complimented my figure, made me feel fabulous. I wanted to text Silk how excited I was to see her, but I knew better not to. I didn't know how she felt about me and I wasn't about to put myself out there.

I slipped on my ankle socks and high-top sneakers. I picked up my purse and keys with a swoop. I went to my mother's bedroom and pulled out my denim jacket out of the closet. The back of the jacket had a heart painted on it from an artist who lived near my community garden. After he painted it, he told me to only wear it during the days I was nervous but excited about an unknown experience. Kudos to Greg the painter.

I texted Silk that I was on my way and walked over to the liquor store to pick up the Rosé. When I got on the L train, my belly was in shambles. I continued to focus on my breaths so I wouldn't vomit on my new outfit and the man's suitcase who was sitting beside me. The entire ride was twenty minutes, but it felt like five. I got off the train and walked slowly to the exit stairs. I scanned the entire station and found no one that looked like Silk. My phone buzzed in my bag and I knew it was Silk:

I'm running a little late. I'm only two stops away.

I had no complaints. I walked up the steps and texted her back okay. I dug into my bag for my compact mirror and reapplied my lip gloss. I paused once I heard the clanging of metal, screeches and hot air pushing against my face. I saw the train lights and fumbled to place my lip gloss into my bag. I walked up the second flight of stairs to the outside and shoved the mirror in my bag. I posed at least four times, hoping to find the best, *I look real good standing here waiting for you to arrive, but it's not a big deal* stance. I counted to thirty hoping I'd see her head bopping up and down as she went up the steps. By the time I reached twenty-nine, I saw at least twenty strangers leave the station. I pulled out my phone and was beginning to text Silk to find out where she was until I heard her voice, "I hope you weren't waiting long."

My chest was on fire. My tummy felt as though various strings of thread were doing a snake dance. I smiled, she smiled, and I timidly placed my phone in my bag.

"No, not too long. I arrived about ten minutes ago. Hey, Silk," I replied as I wrapped my arms around her.

The nerves melted away. The threads fell to the bottom of my stomach and my chest was calm. I felt at ease. She smelled like frankincense and myrrh. She just had her cornrows done. So many designs and shine, I was in awe.

"I like your hair. You just had it done?"

"I'm glad you like it, Ms. Roxy. I got it done yesterday. Needed something new. you know?

I nodded.

We made small talk about our hair and how we take care of our hair individually. The venue was only seven blocks away from the train station, but it felt like three when we walked it together. It was a grocery store that turned into a small musical venue for independent artists and bands. "Velvet Bodega" flashed consistently, and I gagged to myself at the name.

"Velvet bodega. Really?" I said aloud.

"Yep, it's a bodega for the bougie folk like us, Ms. Roxy."

We both laughed and observed the building. It was obviously her first time, too, by the way she slowed down once we reached the security guard in front of the venue.

As the orange light flashed on the three of us, the security guard gave us a wince and said, "Hello, welcome to Velvet Bodega. You with Gia?"

"Nah, but we're here for her show," Silk replied.

He checked his watch and shook his head. "Too early. I'm only letting in the band and workers. I let folks in at about 7:30."

"Okay, sounds good. Thanks." Silk smiled.

He smiled right after her. Silk looked at me and said, "There's a bar a block up. Let's get some drinks—on me."

"Sure," I replied.

Now I have to find some more topics to talk about and be interesting.

"So, are you far from this spot?" Silk asked.

"Nah, not at all. The walk to the L train wasn't bad and neither was the train ride. What about you, Silk?"

"Hell yeah, Ms. Roxanne." We both chuckled.

She continued, "Coming from Queens, it was a journey for sure. I took the bus to the E train and had to deal with the usual shenanigans on that train. You know how that goes."

I gave her a blank stare.

She raised her eyebrow and sighed.

We reached the bar, and Silk reached around me to open the door for me.

"Thanks, Silk."

"Of course."

We sat at the bar and scanned the room. It was just us and two elderly friends at the back of the bar.

I blindly felt underneath the bar table for a hook to put my bag on. Silk joined me on the search. Our fingers brushed against each other as we felt the metal curve. My breath slowed down and my cheeks felt hot. I quickly glanced in her eyes only to find her returning the quick gaze.

"Sorry about that."

"No worries. Thanks for helping me look."

"For you? Of course," she said as she smiled.

I observed her outfit and facial expression as she waved her hand to get the bartender's attention. She wore a white hooded t-shirt, which was snug against her breasts. Topping it off was a black denim jacket. I loved her black baggy jeans. Her thighs were thick, and she chose jeans that complimented them well yet still had enough space to fill everywhere else.

"Hey, man. How you doing?"

"I'm good, thanks. So, what'll it be?"

"Lemme get a Stella on tap and she'll have..."

Her lips looked soft. I watched them intently, as her voice was on cool, calm and collected. I wonder what kind of Chapstick uses to—

"Hey, Roxy, what would you like?"

"Oh, yeah. Yes, I'd like a cranberry and house vodka. How much is it?" I asked.

"Don't worry about it, I got you, Shawty," Silk said.

I was trying to say thanks, but I'm sure my hot cheeks said enough.

"So anyway, about that E train you don't seem to know nothing about," she said.

"Well, I've taken it a few times to Queens Plaza mall," I replied.

Our drinks hit the table, and the bartender wished us a good sipping.

"Nah. Then you don't know. I will say, the homelessness in our city is a damn shame. I used to volunteer at this soup kitchen in Harlem, and you wouldn't believe the stories I heard. People with full-time jobs yet they can't afford to rent a studio."

"Of course not," I interjected.

"The rent is ludicrous, and the minimum wage has remained the same. The working poor. Craziness, Silk."

"Yep, there definitely needs to be some solutions to this problem. Million-dollar lofts with only three people living in them. Something has to be done. The homelessness in NYC is unfortunate. But I don't know how much longer I can take of the bum cologne and live-in train cars."

I almost choked on my cranberry and vodka upon hearing that. "Bum cologne? What?" I cackled.

"Yeah! Especially during the winter when they have nowhere to go. They sleep on the E train and carry their things with them. I don't blame them. Gotta keep warm. But, damn, Roxy, that bum cologne is strong. Phew."

We were both chuckling and slapping the bar.

"You are so silly, Silk."

Finally catching her breath, she continued, "Oh man. Listen, I've had my rough times, too. I've slept in my car when I was living in Chicago for a short spell. I understand, but damn. Sometimes, when the E train is pulling in and I see like two cars empty while the others are crowded, I take my ass right into that crowded one. I will not disrespect my nose on my way to work. Nope."

More laughter erupted from our section, and the elderly duo were now smiling and watching us. The bartender chuckled to himself as he wiped down the other side of the bar table.

"You really sat up here and said bum cologne. What am I gonna do with you?" I asked as I took another sip of my drink.

She glanced at me, gulped down the rest of her beer, knocked on the bar table, and winked at me. "I can think of a couple things, Ms. Roxy."

I needed to hear her utter that again. "Huh?"

She raised her glass towards the bartender, and she walked over to us.

"Ready for another glass?" the bartender asked.

She winked and smiled at me.

As we talked about my job, Shelly, and how I'm looking to work elsewhere, I felt so at home with her. I felt safe to whisper my secrets in her hand and confident that she would simply cup them and slip them in her pocket.

Silk's phone alarm went off and we headed back to the venue to see Gia perform. Once we got our hands stamped and walked into the venue, I was stunned. It was huge compared to what it looked like on the outside. It was dark with speckled red and purple lights all throughout the place. There were bleachers in the back and three rows of black velvet chairs. Silk guided us to the front row, and we sat farthest to the right. A few people walked up to Silk and made small talk while I sheepishly sat there. Waiting for her to introduce me, I eventually sunk back into my seat and pulled out my phone. I got the hint. We're just acquaintances and it will stay that way because she didn't introduce me. *She has no romantic feelings for me. Got it.*

"And who's this gorgeous lady you brought with you?" one of her friends chimed in my direction.

"My name is Roxy, and you?"

"Diana. I love your romper. How lovely."

"Thanks, Diana."

Silk remained quiet as Diana and I spoke while her other friends observed us. When they returned back to their seats, Silk smiled at me and looked down at the ground. I was trying to translate the awkward silence. Was she shy now that it was just us surrounded by familiar faces? Does she secretly have a girlfriend? Is she testing-

"Hey, did you bring alcohol?" she inquired as she wrapped her hand on my knee softly and squeezed gently. My heart fluttered as it rose up slowly to my neck. I nodded and looked into her eyes. She dived into my own and we breathed together for a few moments. *Have I met her before? Those eyes feel like home and I know that she knows it.*

I watched her mouth opened as her perfectly white teeth revealed themselves.

"Roxy?" There goes that grin again.

"Oh."

I dug into my bag and pulled out the bottle of Rosé. She pulled out a sandwich bag that contained two plastic cups.

"Well, aren't you innovative," I teased.

"I'm glad you think so," she replied as she nudged my forearm.

I poured the drinks while she held the cups.

"What will we toast to?" she asked.

"To new experiences?" I nervously smiled

She closed her eyes, inhaled, and said, "To fresh and authentic connections."

We tapped each other's plastic cups and made small talk about music venues we'd been to. After about ten minutes, the host walked on the wooden stage and requested for everyone to be seated. He introduced Gia who was decked out in gold: gold jeans, gold button down, gold pumps and a red bow tie. Even her eyelashes were gold. I was mesmerized by her entire presentation. She sat on a red stool and spoke about the makings of her musical project and what inspired her. Every few moments, I would sneak glances at Silk. Her eyes glittered from the speckled lights and Gia's movements. Once Gia began to sing, my entire focus was on her voice. It was almost as if my late grandmother was singing wisdom to me. It was so welcoming and distinct.

∞

After the performance, I chatted with a few people while Silk took pictures with her friends. I didn't want to intrude or appear desperate to be close to her. We both looked at each other and instinctively knew we were ready to leave. She nodded her head up, I returned the nod and raised my cup. We walked and looked around silently.

"You takin' the L train, Ms. Roxanne?"

"You can call me Roxy."

"Cool. Roxy it is…. Ms. Roxanne."

I couldn't help but roll my eyes and smile.

We walked to the train saying nothing but releasing smiles, simpers, and random chuckles. Once we reached the L train station, stopped at the stairs.

"Well, it was nice to see you, Roxy."

I didn't wanna leave yet. I needed more time with her.

I scanned the various restaurants, but I wasn't hungry. I looked around for parks and found nothing.

"I don't wanna leave yet, Silk."

Silk's smile was big. Real big. She quickly shrugged, dropped the smile and replied, "Okay, well we can walk around."

"Talk about everything and nothing?"

"We can do whatever you want, Roxy."

∞

An hour and a half later, we reached the borderline between Queens and Brooklyn. It felt like twenty minutes passed by as we spoke about our past artistic projects, future ones, and mutual creatives we know. She was working on a documentary about indie artists from Chicago who moved to New York and how they had thrived here. We discussed how gentrification had pushed our favorite stores and eateries out for more bland and expensive ones. I felt as if I was talking to my best friend. As we walked back to the L train, we reviewed Gia's show and agreed that it was phenomenal. Silk made sure to mention how she would love to hear me sing on a stage again. Maybe. Hopefully. As the light from the L train stairs glistened on the concrete, I chewed a few ideas for us to extend this moment together, but I had to go home. The soles of my feet were finally beginning to burn. She walked me down the stairs, waited for the train with me, and got on with me.

As the cool air hit our skin I asked, "This isn't out of your way?"

As we leaned on the closed train doors, she shifted her body towards me, gazed into my eyes and replied, "It will never be out of my way to escort you home at least fifty percent of the way. Ever."

I was beaming. I pressed my lips together and nodded.

"Thanks," was all I could say.

We walked off the train at the Lafayette station and she walked me to the exit staircase. She had sadness in her eyes. *Does she like me? Did she not want this night to end either?*

"We should do this again."

"Of course, Ms. Roxanne," she murmured.

There I went beaming again. I wrapped one arm around her neck as she wrapped her arm around the middle of my torso. A wonderful impersonal side hug. We said our goodbyes, and I ran up the steps.

The bus arrived within minutes, and I was grateful. It was a shady bus stop and my yellow romper stuck out. When I found a seat, I texted Silk to let her know that I got on the bus. I noticed that I had a text since 8pm. It was from Johnson.

Hey, Queen. I just want you to know that I love you and we must meet up tomorrow evening. It's an emergency. Hit me up tomorrow meeting so I can tell you where we're meeting.

Oh, brother.

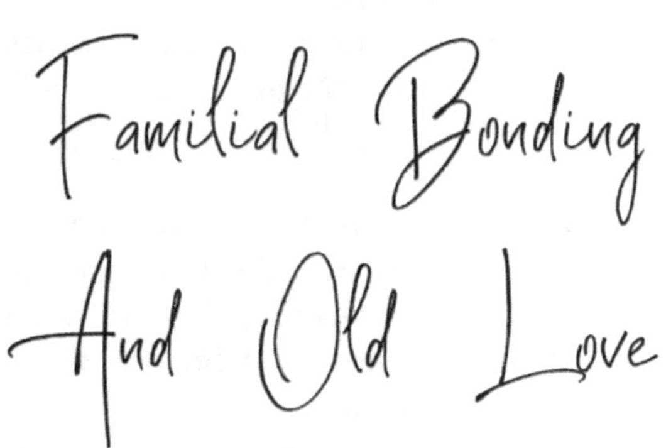

As soon as I arrived home last night, I dropped my bag on the couch and let my body crash into my bed. I woke up to the smell of French toast, syrup, and bacon. I opened my eyes to find my sheet over me and my denim jacket still wrapped around my waist.

For the first time in a while, I woke up excited to start my day. I began humming a song in my head I wanted to write down. The humming eventually transformed into me harmonizing and riffing. "And I found a love everlasting in Greenpoint." My head began to sway as I wiggled my hips to the beat in my head.

"Well, look who is up and singing," Mama called from the kitchen.

"Yeah, I got a song in my head. I got to play it out and sing it before I forget it," I replied. I didn't get out of bed though.

"Well, I hope it's a good song."

"It's about finding love in a new place that's really a familiar place."

"Huh? So, how is it a new place then, Roxanne?"

"It initially feels new, but that's because that love hasn't been felt in so long that it feels new."

"Okay, Honey."

I shook my head and got out of bed.

"You were out late. Who you was with? Annlea and Maggie?"

"No, I was hanging out with someone else."

"It bet' not be that Johnson boy."

"No, Ma'am."

I walked in the kitchen and pecked her on the cheek. "Can I have some?" I squealed.

"Sure," she smiled.

"The ingredients are all in this here kitchen. You can cook yours when I'm done in here."

I winced at her and crossed my arms.

She was her own comedian. She was laughing for at least a minute.

"I made some for the both of us. Get the orange juice out. I'm taking my breakfast to go."

"Where you going?"

"It's April 25th, girl. I have a plane to catch. I'm going to Chicago to preach at Reverend Duncan's church."

"What you glowin' and smilin' like that for? You wanna come?" she teased as she continued stirring the grits in the pot, anticipating some prodigal daughter moment.

"No, I just know someone who lived in Chicago once for a spell," I said as I grabbed the spatula from the counter and slid it under the French toast that sat deliciously on the skillet. I scooped the two pieces up and placed them in my hand. I pulled a plate from out of the cabinet as I had a flashback of last night's walk around Greenpoint with Silk. I giggled to myself remembering her bit about bum cologne. She was so silly. I closed the cabinet door and saw Mama with her hand on her hip and eyebrow raised.

"What you so happy about this morning? What's up with you?"

"Nothing. Just happy. Besides, it's Saturday and I get to relax and create some music."

She pressed her lips together firmly. She looked me up and down, waiting for me to cave in. "Mmhm. I know you hiding somethin'. I'm your mother. Remember that."

"Yes, Mama."

I took two pieces of bacon from the aluminum pan she had on the counter. I grabbed a fork and a knife from the dish rack. I slid out of the kitchen and sat at the table. Mama began humming to herself. An old gospel song that I used to sing as a child with the children's choir. I began to hum with her, remembering the time Tori and I held hands while we swayed side to side, singing the "Prayer of Jabez." We'd been sandwiched between the younger kids in front of us and the older kids behind us. We'd squeeze each other's hand whenever we'd reach parts of the song that was a bit too high for us.

I hadn't seen Tori since I was fourteen years old. Her mother still attended the same church I grew up in. Her mother told me a year before I left the church that Tori got married to a man in Japan. She told me that she has hope for me. I remember her grabbing my hand and patting it lightly saying, "She finally got delivered from that spirit of homosexuality. Thankfully, that spirit didn't snatch you up along with her when ya'll were younger. Y'all were so close." She flashed her three silver front teeth.

"I'm surprised you still remember that song, Roxanne."

"Of course, Mama. How could I forget. Jerry drilled that song into our heads."

We both giggled until she paused to look at her wristwatch.

"Jesus, I gotta get outta here. Wrap this up for me while I get ready."

I watched her fly back to her bedroom to get dressed. I placed her breakfast into two Tupperware bowls and returned to my plate for my last few bites. Leaving my plate on the table, I went into my bag to get my phone. I had six unread messages from Annlea and Maggie asking about last night. I texted them that I would video call them when Mama left. I put my plate in the sink and hopped in the shower.

Last night's adventure still made my skin tingle and my cheeks rise. I was shimmying in the shower to Gia's music in my head. I felt at ease with Silk. I didn't need my guards up. I didn't have to protect myself. I spoke about my music and was listened to. She was so cool and down to earth. Hot damn those thick thighs though. Mama swung open the door, disturbing my daydream of walking with Silk through Prospect Park.

She snatched the shower curtain open and kissed me on the cheek.

"Alright, Roxanne, I'm heading out. I will text you when I land. I should be home by Monday night. Behave and act like you got some sense."

"Yes, Mama. You could've at least knocked."

"Chile, please. This is my house you living in."

She kissed me once more, pulled the curtain forward and told me that she loved me.

"I love you, too," I yelled out. I heard the door slam and continued my daydream.

As soon as I got out the shower, towel wrapped around my body, shower cap still on, I video called Annlea and Maggie. I told them every single detail about last night and Annlea squealed along with me. Maggie was excited for me too. Annlea left the call to return back to work. She was the head manager at Follie, a boutique for plus-sized men. Maggie had to go a few minutes later to catch the Amtrak. Once again, she was traveling out of town.

I got dressed and scrolled through PicMyBiz. I stopped at Silk's picture she posted this morning. It was the picture she took with her friends last night at Velvet Bodega. I liked it and almost commented on it but stopped myself just in time. Can't have her thinking I like her or something.

I swept all the floors in the apartment and got ready to watch a few videos on my laptop until my song returned to my head. I ran behind the couch and pulled out my keyboard. Mama had saved up her money to purchase a Yamaha keyboard for me during my senior year in high school. I started taking lessons at age nine and stopped at age sixteen. The lessons had gotten a bit pricey. I learned enough to make my own music, which is all I care about anyway.

I sat on the couch with the keyboard in my lap. There were speckles of lint on the keys. I traced my fingers on a few of the keys and hummed the song. I went in the kitchen to get a wipe and clean my keys. Once I got resettled, I turned on the keyboard and pressed my finger down on the middle C. I began to play the notes to the song in my head. Twenty minutes later, I had the first verse and the chorus. I fetched my song book and wrote my new song. I sang aloud acapella as I danced in front of the couch. I sang it a few more times until I got comfortable with the lyrics swirling around on my tongue. I leaped. I skipped around the small apartment until I was out of breath. I sat at the table and was about to text Annlea and Maggie to ask if they'd like to hear my song, but they're both preoccupied. I texted Johnson about making a new song and asking if he wanted to hear it. I needed somebody to hear my song. Thirty minutes went by and I was on my couch watching videos on my laptop about various singers I admire. I texted Johnson to meet me at the Prospect Park entrance at 3pm. He replied back "K" within moments. He wanted to meet up with me about some so-called emergency anyway. I closed my eyes, held my breath and tapped the numbers. As I put my ear to the phone, I knew that if she picked up, I would play the best that I could.

"Hello?"

"Hey, Karla. It's Roxy."

"Oh, snap. It's good to hear from you. Yo, I found out that the coffee spot in Bay ridge is still open. Remember the one we used to go to when we were together?"

"Oh, yeah. I remember. We almost got kicked out after arguing with that old white lady who told us we were walking abominations."

"Yep, ya crazy ass had your tongue all down my throat and your hand down my pants. You told her to leave us alone or we'll put on a show for her. We sure did put on a show didn't we, Rox?"

"Sure did. Listen, I wrote a song and—"

"—Let me hear it then. I'm glad you wrote a new song."

I held the phone to my chest as I shrieked.

"Okay, hold on."

I sat on the couch, placed the keyboard on my lap, and sat my phone on the top of my keyboard.

"Can you hear me, Karla?"

"I can hear you."

My fingertips danced on the keyboard as I closed my eyes and sang. When I finished, I heard Karla clapping through the phone.

I scooched the keyboard from my lap and picked up my phone. As I spun around the living room, I asked, "So what do you think?"

"I love it. I can't wait until you finish it. It's fresh and soulful. Wonderful love song. The melody is not too complicated either. You should be proud of yourself. You've come along way, Roxanne. So have I."

"How so?"

"Well, after seeing you at Serene's Coffee Shop I realized just how stupid it was to let you get away. Then when I saw you on stage singing and doing what you love, my heart wanted to leap onto the stage and love on you."

"Karla, I just called for your ear to hear my new music 'cause you always kept it real with me. Where is this conversation going?"

"This conversation is going towards my heart. I need you back, Rox. How could you not see it? I came to your play and supported you. I missed you so much and I am so sorry for letting you get away. Listen Roxy, you're the most beautiful—"

"—Let me cut you off right there. I appreciate you listening to my new song. Thank you and I'm glad you opened your heart to me and got all vulnerable. But what's over, is over."

"But Roxy, I know this time that—"

"—You're a wonderful woman. You're smart, kind, funny, attractive, witty, strong, focused and sociable. You will find your person for sure. But I need you to know it ain't me. I think you and I should stay good friends, though."

Karla was quiet for a moment. "I hear you, Rox. I respect your decline and compliments and all. Later, Roxy."

My heart was racing. My stomach felt heavy.

"Karla—"

She hung up.

She texted me that there is a showcase that I should audition for. If I get featured, I'll be paid $200 to perform. I texted her back thanks.

Going Backwards

I met with Johnson at a park bench deep within Prospect Park. I arrived there an hour earlier so I could write some songs and enjoy nature. Annlea and Maggie were still too busy to hear my song and I needed another set of ears to hear it. Might as well put Johnson to some use.

Even in sweats and an oversized white t-shirt, I felt like royalty. My skin was moisturized, I used a facial scrub I purchased in Miami and felt refreshed. I wore a pair of white flip flops so my feet could get some sun and feel the grass for a few minutes before meeting Johnson.

When I received his text that he arrived, I walked over to the bench and waited for his arrival. He wore a maroon tight button-down, short sleeve top with gray trousers. Like me, he wore a pair of flip flops. As he got closer to me, he decelerated his steps. Forecasting my brown arms to raise up and reach out to him, he was met with my butt still on the park bench. My lips pressed firmly together, he stopped a foot in front of me and crossed his arms.

"Hey."

He looked at me for a few minutes and replied, "This is not how we do things, and you know that, Roxy. Get your ass up and hug me, Queen."

"You can bring your ass over here on this park bench. I ain't your woman."

"Oh, I see. You do some janky-ass play full of fags and weirdos and now you're feeling yourself."

I looked into his eyes and saw it. The need to rile me up.

"You are forgetting that I, too, date women, have loved women, and am attracted to women. Also, from what I recall, you occasionally like men so—"

Johnson ran to my side, plopped his butt on the park bench and growled, "That was only once, and I don't have feelings like that anymore. I already told you that I got the Holy Ghost when I was at church and since then, I don't have those damn feelings."

I couldn't help but chuckle. "Okay, well anyway. Keep your offensive slurs about who I am to yourself," I replied.

"I didn't call you that I said janky ass play full of—"

"Say it again and I'll leave."

I was ready to go.

He leaned away from me, pressed his hand to his chest and raised his eyebrows. He sure can put on a show.

"Well, somebody can't take a joke."

"Humor is subjective. Next."

Johnson sat back, looked ahead, and crossed his arms again. Serving me a few stank looks, I was in awe at the antics.

Watching a few birds play in the grass in front of us, he cut through the silence and asked, "So how have you been?" He shifted his body to face me and uncrossed his arms. "Really?"

"I took myself shopping, got a massage, got a manicure and a pedicure, wrote some new music, hung out with friends, and Silk and I went to see an indie artist called Gia. She was wonderful. It was fun hanging out with Silk. What the hell is the damn emergency you mentioned via text?"

The breeze, rustling of trees and children laughing from a distance replied to me initially.

He pulled out his phone and began to play a game.

"Well, my co-worker, Lanisha is wonderful. She has a great body and she's a great cook. But I want you to know that I love you, Roxy."

I nodded, looking past his face. He began to grin and continued, "But I am not in love with you."

I rose up and looked into his eyes. I turned to the left and walked ahead. I felt lighter. With each step, I was further away from him and it was as if the wind was blowing away the heaviness on my shoulders. I took a deep breath and exhaled in relief.

There was this burrito place that Silk once mentioned to me that I should try. *I think I'll go there to treat myself.* I heard footsteps running towards me. I shuffled into my sweat pocket for my red pocketknife. With my hand still in my pocket, I gripped the knife and waited 'til the running steps got closer.

Tap, tap, thud

I swung around, ready to pull out my knife, only to relax once seeing Johnson.

"Hey."

He slid his hands to his knees as he tried to catch his breath. *The fuck does he want now?*

He slowly pulled his shirt up a little and said, "Does Silk like you?"

"No, I don't think so."

She didn't introduce me to her friends, she gave me a mutual friendly hug and never flirted. Yet, neither have I.

Johnson looked into my eyes and searched. For what? I didn't care.

"Maybe the love is still there. This break has messed things up for us and maybe it did more damage than good. This break has caused my feelings to be out of sorts. Let's maybe try again."

My heart screamed *NO*. My phone vibrated three times, which meant that my mother texted me.

"Hold on. That's Mama."

I pulled out my phone, turned my back to Johnson and took two steps away from him.

Roxanne. Church went great. The anointing was heavy in that church. Do me a favor and pick up some flour and eggs. I want to make pancakes as soon as I arrive home.

I sucked in my jaw and began to tap my foot. I live under her roof still. Guess I'll pick up what she wants on my way back home.

"Fine, Johnson. Let's see if this works."

If Mama finds out I like women, I'm sure my ass would hit the curb hard.

∞

Later on that night, we went to Shaveè Hotel in lower Manhattan. The man at the front desk had a name tag that read "Silk." My heart fluttered, and I flashed him a smile as he handed Johnson a card holder with two hotel keys. The room was spacious, spotless, and chic. I wanted to hide in the closet by the window and hopefully vanish. But I had to be here.

I told him I was going to take a shower while he went downstairs to get us some snacks and check out the takeout spot across the street. I let the water settle my thoughts for a few moments. I waited for the main issue to come from the attic of my mind and out of my lips.

"I want out of this."

I let truth overcrowd the bathroom and stand with me for a while. I dried off and put on my pajamas. I thought about holding Silk's hand while walking across the boardwalk with her. I heard footsteps by the door and quickly hurried to the bed. The door didn't open, so I turned on the television and saw two women at an altar wearing white. I smiled at the thought of those two women being Silk and I. I heard the hotel door close and Johnson's voice booming, "What the fuck is this?"

I quickly sat up, clenched my toes, and held my breath. I attempted to push out words, but anxiety taped my mouth shut once he marched towards me. He snatched the remote from my hands and turned the channel to a station that only aired cartoons.

"This is more like it."

"I was watching that."

He scoffed and waved me off. "It was garbage anyway," he replied.

So much for celebrating a fresh commitment and giving this a second chance. We're off to a splendid start.

He went to the bathroom, and I texted Silk goodnight. I turned off the lights and left the lamp on for Johnson. I let sleep hold my eyelids captive and drift into the darkness until I heard blaring, punching sounds. I jolted my eyes open and looked at the anime battle that was on television. Johnson turned his head towards me, looked into my eyes, and shrugged. I thought about Silk's breasts in a fitted hoodie, and my heart rose. I shook my head and slid my hands down Johnson's plaid boxers. I added pressure with my fingertips and slowed down once I heard him moan. I imagined my back arched and Silk's head between my legs. I exhaled softly and gave a side grin to wishful thoughts. Nipples erect and toes curled, Johnson chuckled.

"Somebody wants a taste."

With his eyes still fixated on the television screen, a crooked smile was painted on his face. He sighed and struggled to lift his hand above my breast. He cupped it lightly, then swiped my nipple with his index finger like a touch screen kiosk. I rolled my eyes at the lackluster embrace and turned my back to him. I fell back asleep and saw her again. She was standing on a bridge. Her afro swayed wildly in the wind as she looked out at the river before her. I watched her chest rise and sink into her baggy blue T-shirt. I was standing at the beginning of the bridge, waiting for her to look my way. She was waiting for me. I pressed my bare toes onto the wooden bridge. I took another step forward until I felt my arm being yanked backwards. My head fell back, and I felt my chest stutter continuously. Eyes black and cornrows slithering like serpents, Johnson hissed. He gripped my arm tighter and wrapped himself around me.

"You belong to me, damn it," he grunted

I heard her voice whisper, "I'm right here, Shawty."

I flipped open my eyes and remained stiff. It was completely dark in the hotel room, and Johnson's arms were snuggled around my small frame. He pressed his lips heavily on my cheek and squeezed me tighter.

"Shh, I got you," he cooed.

I wanted to yell. Why was that just a dream? Her arms should've been wrapped around me, not his. I rolled my eyes in the room that was coated in black. What if liking Silk was just some silly phase? I've only liked her for few months. Johnson's not perfect, but when things are good, life is manageable.

His hand glided up my pajama top, and he cupped the bottom of my breast. *This method again*. I wanted to feel Silk's breast pressed against my back. I wanted to quiver from her erect nipples kissing my skin. Johnson doesn't have breast. Silk does.

I wiggled from his grip and straddled on his waist. I walked my fingers up his torso and let my fingertips read his chest like braille. I ceased reading his physique when I reached his areolas. I arched my spine as I slide down to his thighs. Hand anchored down to the bed; I fixed my body, ready to taste his nipples. If only they were Silk's breasts. I made circles around his nipples with my tongue. Silk's face canvased my mind as my hand voyaged for his boxers. Fumbling over the shape of his cock, I rubbed his shaft through his boxers slowly until he surrendered a moan.

I bit my lip as I envisioned Silk's fingertips trickling over my hips, dripping towards my mid-section. *Damn, I adore her cheekbones*. The way she clenched her jawline when she's in deep thought or concentration makes breathing waver… a little. My tongue journeyed down to his belly button and returned to his chest. If only Johnson had breasts. I'd love to have something to gently press between my hands. I felt my head jerk up and Johnson parting his legs wide.

"You've been up there for too damn long, Roxy. What do you think you're doing licking my pecs for thirty damn minutes?"

His hands still on my forehead, I sat up on his hips and smacked his hands off my head. I wanted to hurl in the darkness as I gripped his cock. I released it, jumped off the bed, and walked over to the window. I opened the curtains and looked back at the moonlight spotlighting his mid-section. I took a deep breath and closed my eyes. It will be over before I know it. So, the sooner I do this, the sooner it will be over.

I dragged my feet to the bed and laid my body to the side. I took another deep inhale and exhaled slowly. I sat on my knees and glared at his moonlit dick as though it were a used scalpel at a doctor's office. I craved Silk's smooth suede brown skin kissing mine. I swear I smelled her scent for a millisecond as I held Johnson's cock with both hands. Knees spread apart and ready for the conclusion of this, I sunk my head to his dick and licked it. It tasted like salt, un-showered skin, and unseasoned chicken cutlets. I gripped it tighter and engulfed him in my mouth. I hope this time will be short.

He came in under five minutes, and I exhaled quietly. I jumped off the bed and rinsed my mouth out. I don't swallow, but the taste of his skin made my tongue feel disappointed. The slit of the moonlight helped me find my purse to retrieve the baby wipes. I pulled out three wipes and threw them on his stomach as I plopped back on the bed next to him. He let the wipes lay on his six-pack abs for a moment. I watched the wipes rise and fall with him in silence. He snatched the wipes from his stomach and slowly wiped off his own ejaculation. I listened to his breathing until he spoke up.

"You finally made me cum from head and not sex. You don't seem too excited about that."

I heard his pillow crinkle. I knew he was looking at me. I didn't respond. I couldn't. I didn't give a damn if he ejaculated or not. I abhor giving head, but that's what a partner is supposed to do: please their partner. I am committed to make sure all areas are covered, even if certain areas make me hurl.

He chucked the wipes on the floor and sighed heavily. He sat up and kissed my forehead, then sat in front of me with his legs open. He gripped my ankles gently and pushed them forward. I watched my knees rise, and I visualized Silk's face smiling at me in the moonlight instead of his. I felt his hands slide up the sides of my legs and met each other at my kneecaps. He parted my legs open and thumbed my clit softly. I didn't move. His thumb pressed in and out until I jolted.

"Ouch, slow down, damn it," I screamed.

He apologized and lowered his head. I looked up at the darkness as I felt his tongue petting my pussy. I'm sure my vagina didn't have a tail. It certainly doesn't meow. He stopped now and then to hear any moans. My throat, lips, and sensuality were silent. He eventually realized his tongue was doing nothing but soaking up a bed and an unbothered vagina. He sighed, and I watched his face rise in the moonlight with a half-smile. With lowered eyes and a wink, he said, "I've got more for you, Roxy."

Hopefully, he'll be done in ten minutes. I want to go to sleep. He held my legs up in the air and went to work; I guess. The penetration was actually getting good until he let me know he was about to cum.

"Already?" I replied. "That was quick."

Johnson said nothing. He slammed his body next to me.

"Um, Johnson, I have your cum on my belly."

He whined and got up. He walked over to my bag to retrieve a baby wipe and wiped his mess off my stomach. He threw the wipe on the floor and plopped back on the bed. He leaned over to kiss me, but I turned my body and sat up on the bed. I walked over to the bathroom and stood in front of the doorway for a few minutes.

I could never make Johnson cum simply form oral sex. I finally did tonight, and I didn't care. I stood at the doorway, searching in the darkness for the feeling that made me stay with him for this long. *Obligation,* I mouthed. I entered the bathroom and cleaned myself off at the sink. When I walked back out and saw Johnson's body clear with the slit of the moonlight, something within me stopped. I swear to God when my eyes reached his chest, something sank into my stomach and remained there. I dragged my feet to the bed and slid under the sheets. With my body facing Johnson's, I glared at his eyelashes that clapped continuously towards the ceiling. I placed the palm of my hand on his chest and breathed in deeply, hoping to inhale the same infatuation I've had for Karla, Patricia, or Silk. Nothing.

"Goodnight," I whispered into his ear.

"Night, Baby," he replied.

Eyes wide open, he sighed softly, and I gave into the lost love and slumber.

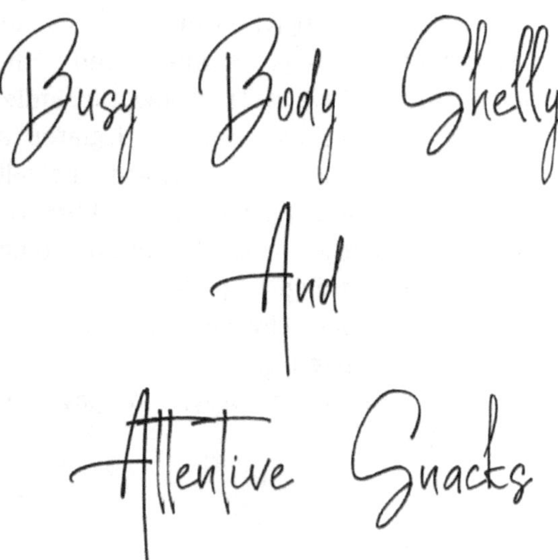

I sat at my desk, pretending to type something at the computer as my boss, Nichelle, passed by my cubicle.

"Hey, Roxy, how's it going?" she asked as she leaned on my cubicle.

"Pretty good. It's a slow day," I replied.

"Yes, I know. That's why I'm here. We're all going home by twelve. I think our team effort to catch up on Friday was a bit too productive," she chuckled.

I made sure to release a phony laugh, too.

"Sounds good. Do you need anything done?"

"Um...No. No one was absent last week, so there aren't any absent notices. Just make sure there aren't any files out. If so, just put them away, okay?"

I nodded. "Got it, Nichelle."

She tapped my cubicle lightly and walked off. I texted Silk good morning, and she texted it back. She asked me how I was doing, and I told her that I was good but was craving skittles. She didn't respond. I shrugged it off and walked over to Shelly's cubicle. I knocked on the back of her chair, and she jolted forward. She spun her chair around, eyes wide and mouth open. When she saw my face, she slouched back into her seat

"Girl, you scared me. I thought you was Nichelle. She told you that we're leaving early, right?"

"Yep. Thank goodness because there wasn't much for me to do. One more hour and we outta here," I said, as I raised my hand for Shelly to give me a high five.

She slapped my hand and smiled. "Thank goodness. My ass needs it. I went to this brotha's hotel, and he wore me the hell out."

My phone was vibrating consistently. "Oh, hold on, Shelly."

I pulled my phone out from my back pocket and saw Silk's name flashing.

"Silk," I said aloud to myself.

"Who this Silk person that got you smilin' like that?"

"None of your business." I smiled.

She clutched her air pearls and gasped. "Well, excuse me. Well, Roxanne anyway, I hope it ain't—"

I turned my back to her, walked quickly down the row of cubicles as I put the phone to my ear and I rushed out the Human Resources door.

"Hey, Silk. Hold on."

There was a burgundy couch to the left of me where I had spent many mornings, munching on my breakfast before starting my shift. I anchored my booty on the couch and caught my breath.

"Hello?"

"Hey, Roxy. Sorry for calling you during your shift. I won't do it again. I just wanted to know if you want to meet up and just chill for a bit."

"Oh okay, yeah. Sounds good. I'm leaving in like an hour anyway. It's really slow here at work. I'll go home, change my clothes, and we can meet up at the Trader Bob's downtown."

"The one near Court Street?"

"Yep, that's the one. How about we meet there at 3pm?"

"Sounds good to me, Roxy."

"Cool." I smiled.

We hung up, and I sat on the burgundy couch for a few seconds. My body melted into my seat as I thought about what I would wear to see her. I couldn't wait to catch up with her and update her about what's going on in my life. This was definitely going to be a good two days. *I'll see Silk today and then Dr. Ramsey tomorrow.* I got up from the couch, swung open the Human Resources office door, and skipped back to my cubicle to get ready to clock out.

∞

I walked slowly once I hopped off the B38. Six blocks away from the Trader Bob's Supermarket, I let the late afternoon breeze waft through my two strand twists. I looked down at my legs and hips as they strut in my red high waisted pants. I had nice legs. I wore a white button-down top that had ruffles around the collar. As my red feather earrings tickled my neck and shoulders, I smiled at how uplifted they made me feel. Annlea had given them to me after the chaotic scene with Johnson at home. She handed it to me and whispered to me, "Congratulations. You didn't give a beast what he wanted."

She embraced me for a long time, and I'm sure I could have cried. I loved my friends.

I texted Silk that I was a block away as I was crossing the street to Trader Bob's Supermarket. I put my phone into my back pocket and waited for it to vibrate. I watched

the faces that passed by me in front of Trader Bob's. Silk
was nowhere in sight, and I was just about to walk further
up the block to get some ice cream. As I walked two steps
to trot on over to Raylene's ice cream, I felt a light brush
against the bottom of my back.

Silk slid in front of me, walking in front me she said,
"Hey there, Shawty. You was really about to leave?"

"Hell yeah," I snarled.

She stopped walking backward raised up her arms in
surrender. "Well, damn I'm sorry. I apologize. I got here
about ten minutes ago to pick up something you wanted."

I raised my eyebrow and crossed my arms. A grin
crept up on my face. "I ain't ask you for nothin', Silk."

"No, but you told me what you wanted."

She dug into her bookbag and pulled out two packs of
skittles. The red pack and the blue one. I snatched them
out of her hand and jerked her body to me so I could wrap
my arms around her neck. Her arms slid around my waist
and she breathed in deeply. She eventually let me go and
shrugged.

"No biggie. It's just Skittles," she said as she looked
everywhere except my eyes.

"Well, thanks, Silk. I appreciate it."

"Of course. If I got it, then I got us."

I knew my cheeks were red, but I didn't care anymore.
I was swooning.

We walked to the Brooklyn bridge Park Pier 5 cracking
jokes, discussing current events and our favorite films.
When we reached the pier, we sat at one of the picnic
tables and sat in silence for a few moments while we
watched people pass by.

I finally broke the silence and said, "So, what's your
deal, Silk?"

"What you mean?"

"I know you are a filmmaker, actor and photographer. I know you spent a few years in Chicago, but you from Queens. What else?"

"Well, I make my money doing photography and filmmaking prizes from various contests. I have four siblings. I'm the oldest. My parents never married, but I'm for marriage. I don't do drugs, but I do drink occasionally. I love to listen to everything. I didn't grow up a charismatic Christian home like you. I was in Chicago because my ex-girlfriend needed to leave NYC. So, I found a nice loft for us in Chicago and thought that I could really establish myself there—"

"—Hold up, what happened with you and that chick? You told me that you were homeless for a while," I interrupted.

"I don't wanna get too deep, but long story short, she left me for someone else. I needed to find a roommate. She was doing some things she had no business doing, so I lost the loft."

"Damn, Silk."

"Yeah," she said, looking out at the water. "What happened to your arm?"

"What you mean?"

She placed her index finger and thumb around my wrist. She turned my wrist around to expose the two scars that ran vertically across.

"Those."

If anyone else would have done that, an outburst would have ensued and a good old-fashioned cuss out. But, with Silk, I felt relaxed. She was curious to know without malicious intent.

"When I was younger, I used to cut. From ages 16-18 then one time at 20 and a full-blown relapse a year ago. But I'm better now."

She nodded and looked into my eyes. "Mmm. I see. No judgements from me. Life gets hard sometimes. Sometimes we don't know how to be who we really are, so we suppress it for a while, but it seeps out in various ways." She lightly stroked where my scars were. She kissed her hand and cocked her head to the side as she placed the kissed hand on my scars.

The water rose up in my eyes, and I was trying my hardest not to let the tears fall. Of course, there was that one rebellious tear that fell fast, but Silk's thumb was faster. She wiped it away softly and apologized.

"I didn't mean to say anything to offend you. Or did I upset you?"

"You did neither. Just had a moment is all. I'm sensitive."

What the fuck did I just admit to her? What is happening right now?

"I feel you. I really do. So, what's your deal with this musical voice you got in them vocals of yours, Shawty?

"Well, my ex, Karla, mentioned to me about this showcase that is paying the artists to perform. I gotta audition for it, but I think I'll get a spot."

"I know you got it, Roxy." She flashed me her gazillion dollar smile and I tried not get too mesmerized by her smooth cheeks.

"You know, I had a moment, when I was homeless in Chicago, I almost committed suicide, but by the grace of God, I'm here. I know you an atheist and all, but I'm not. Without Him, I wouldn't be here."

"I feel you, and I respect that. I'm glad you're still here, too."

Say it, Roxy, don't be scared to say it.

"You're a dope person and I would've hate to have missed out on getting to know you."

"Likewise, Ms. Roxanne."

Her smooth ass. There I was, smiling like I just won three million dollars.

We continued to open up about our parents, childhood memories and childhood traumas. Four hours passed by and the sun was swallowed up by a navy sky. Silk wanted me to sing a song for her that I wrote. I sang to her the song I recently wrote, and she loved it. She even interpreted it perfectly. It was if she was listening to my soul. She requested to hear some more of my music, so I emailed her four songs that I recorded on my phone.

"Thanks for this, Roxy. I can't wait to listen to them. Well, I gotta get ready to roll out. I have an audition in Harlem."

"Where and for what?"

"It's for my friend's play about a woman in an abusive relationship. Her abusive partner is a woman, and she blackmailed the main character to not press charges or else she would out her to her parents. The main character eventually presses charges and she's free."

"Whoa, that's intense."

"Yes, it is. My friend wants to bring awareness to domestic violence that happens within the LGBTQ+ community."

"I dig it. So, what do you want to audition for?"

She pulled up her pants, pushed out her pelvis and shook her shoulders. "The Pappy," she yelled.

I hooted as she pretended to be an old father. We departed ways once we reached the Borough Hall train station. We gave each other the typical side hug, and I watched her go down the station.

Does she like me? She did shrug about giving me the Skittles. She's probably just a smooth boi by default.

When I arrived home, I wrote a whole new song and found the melody to it. I played the song on my keyboard and softly uttered the lyrics. I began writing a second song and eventually pulled out my song book to play some other songs that I haven't shared with anyone. I heard heavy stomping and shook at the scowl on my mother's face.

"I told you about playing that kind of music in my house," she hissed.

I apologized and put the keyboard away. When I got ready for bed, I texted Silk goodnight and she replied back goodnight with a smiley face.

I was excited to spend some time with my father next Friday. He lived in Greenwich, Connecticut with his huge German Shepherd. I loved taking the Metro north and watching the speeding greens, buildings and passing billboards. I always felt like I was taking a miniature vacation going to my father's house. Walking into his home felt as though I was entering a serene temple or a calm home in the south with a roundabout porch and a lemonade pitcher on the railing. Self-acceptance was at his couch as I talked to him about everything and nothing. Healing is in the silence of early mornings in his kitchen cooking. He was my number one person in my life, but ever since I got with Johnson, I kept my distance because I knew how he felt about him. I knew that every time I saw my father, he would make it his business to tell me how much I deserved better. Right now, it didn't matter. I needed to be around him to tell him everything about my life.

The Human Resources department at the library was closed for the rest of the week due to board meetings and position changes with the big wigs. If you weren't a supervisor, you weren't needed. I'm so thankful for just being an administrative assistant. I hummed my songs until I went to sleep and dreamed about singing at Carnegie Hall in a white gown.

Somethings Gotta Be Done

So much for spending quality time with Daddy. He was called into work this morning. Two firefighters were out sick with the stomach flu, so Daddy had to fill in for one of them. At least I had the opportunity to sing my new songs with him on his piano. I had a mini concert for him and Jody, his dog, in his living room. As I played on his custom-made blue Steinway, Jody wagged his tail, and I glanced up a few times at Daddy as he watched me with pride drenched in his eyes.

I told him about Silk and how she's so fun to be around. He gave me no help as to whether or not she might like me back. I didn't have enough information or clues. When I was making pancakes for us, that's when he got the call to go down to the fire station. He kissed me on the forehead and apologized profusely. He told me that I could stay, and we would catch up tomorrow. I was about to accept the offer until I remembered that Johnson and I were supposed to be celebrating our "let's start fresh" commitment. So, after seeing Johnson, I agreed to see Daddy the following morning and the next two days.

I sat on one of the benches in the Greenwich station. The next train wouldn't be for twenty minutes. I received a text from Silk. My tummy felt heavy. I closed her message and looked around the station. I texted my father that I got out of the taxi and was waiting for the 4:30pm train. With a heavy stomach and a fluttering chest, my legs decided to join the tenseness by trembling.

I opened up Silk's message again and read it over multiple times. Thankfully, there was only one person in the waiting area with me who witnessed my minor fit, and he was too ashamed to look at me directly. His eyes would dart from my feet to the clock on the wall. I was rocking back and forth, hoping to get a hold of a summer breeze from the various open windows. I held my breath awaiting an answer from the winds. I'm sure he believed making eye contact with the *crazy lady* was not on his list of things to do in the Greenwich Station waiting area. I was dreading to respond to her text message. I hate when life hits me unexpectantly.

I was on my way to meet up with Johnson and I felt as though my lungs would stop receiving air. I needed answers. We were celebrating this stupid commitment thingy. Sitting in this waiting area now, I realized how significant last night was. The evening Johnson demanded we celebrate this new fresh start; he came face to face with the woman I was crushing on hard. The realization showed its ugly head when I received:

So, I saw your ex two days ago at Charlie's.

I read her text again, four times in four different ways. I even read it aloud while the guy sitting across from me began to fidget. I had to update her that Johnson and I got back together. *What if she has feelings too? I don't want to lose her.*

I looked out into the street to see if a bus was coming. Not one in sight. I sent a video message to Maggie about what Silk texted me. Maggie called me immediately.

"Roxy, I'm trying to understand how in the world you don't see the caution sign that's blinking above your head. Nah, matter of fact, it's been blinking," Maggie's voice boomed from my phone.

I walked out of the waiting room and on to the train platform.

"Well, hello, Maggie," I said.

"Forget all that salutation and greetings, Roxy. The fact that you are so concerned about her feelings more than your own damn boyfriend, is a problem."

I had something slick to say, but I let it sit at the roof of my mouth. She was right, and I was in no position to be defensive about a truth as raw as what she just said. My heart felt as though it was slowly sliding to the bottom of my bubbling stomach.

"You right. I just—I don't know what to do. I mean, I like her a lot and all, but I don't know if she likes me. I just don't want to hurt her..."

Maggie grunted, and I knew she was rolling her eyes at me.

"Roxy, it doesn't matter at this point, because you're not with her. You're with Johnson. I think you need to be honest with yourself and realize that you have a decision to make. Either you leave Silk alone and ya'll stay acquaintances, so you can focus on your relationship with Johnson, or you can drop that poisonous man and keep it pushing. I know you don't know how she feels, but it's clear you gotta do something, Roxanne. This is a problem that will only grow into a monster that will destroy all parties involved, including Silk if she feels just as deeply for you as you do for her."

The train pulled in, and I dragged my feet onto the train.

"I hear you, Maggie. Thanks for being straight with me."

I dropped my butt onto one of the cushioned seats and placed my duffel bag to the seat next to me.

Maggie sighed softly and said, "I just want you to be happy, Roxy."

I felt my chest settle, and I was able to feel the cool air from the air conditioner in between my thighs.

"Thanks, Maggie. I'll update you later. Talk to you some other time."

I hung up my phone and sat back. I thought about the idea of actually being with Silk. I closed my eyes and surrendered to the possibility of being hers. I texted her:

Yea. We got back together a few days ago. ☺

He recently got promoted as an Assistant Manager at Charlie's.

I read the text and stared at it for a while. I hit send and dropped my phone onto my lap. I rested my head on the window. The ride from Connecticut to New York was usually fast. However, today, the journey felt as long as a 1930's country song. My phone jerked me out of my thoughts as it vibrated on my lap. Silk texted me back:

Oh. I didn't know.

I felt like she was disappointed when reading the text message. Could she really be disappointed? That would mean she did have feelings for me? Nah, she didn't even introduce me to her friends. But I can't shake the feeling that maybe she's hurt that I was back with him. I shook my head and texted Johnson that I wasn't coming.

I went back to my father's house.

Brewing

Silk texted me at work that she liked the songs I sent her. She asked me about how my album was doing. I told her that I would call her during my lunch break and tell her about it. I stopped reaching out to Johnson. I was tired of always being the one initiating communication. With that being said, I hadn't heard from him since I saw him last week. He'd uploaded a few pictures of himself on PicMyBiz at a club. Whatever.

Shelly invited to treat me to lunch, but I declined so I could speak to Silk without Shelly eavesdropping on my conversation. 1:00pm couldn't come fast enough. I rushed over to the pizzeria three blocks away from the library and raced over to the Prospect Park, then dialed Silk's number while I searched for an empty park bench. As it rung, I found a bench that was not too far into the park, but just enough to look at the ducks in the pond.

"Hey, Roxy. How you doin', Shawty?"

"I'm good. Thanks for asking about my music earlier."

"Of course, Roxanne. It's your passion. I gotta make sure you're still pursuing what you love."

Tears began to well up in my eyes, but I refused to let them fall. I tilted my head back, letting the water slide back where it came.

"Roxy? You there?"

"I'm here, I'm just um, getting my pizza out of my pizza bag."

I tore open the paper bag and scooped up the pizza with one hand.

"You lying, Roxy?"

"Yes, I was, but I am eating pizza now. I was tearing up a lil' bit because you want to encourage me to pursue my passions. I appreciate that."

"Hm, well I am serious. Well, anyway, I loved that riff you did toward the end of your song, "Memories." The song where you're harmonizing with the saxophone. That was dope. Was that with a live band?"

"Yeah, there was a group I put together of musicians. We literally just jammed. I'd sing and then they'd freestyle a melody to it. We recorded two songs together. It was nice."

"Well, the finished product is phenomenal."

"Thanks, Baby—I mean, Silk."

I stopped chewing and almost hung up the phone.

Silk didn't skip a beat, "You're welcome, Ms. Roxanne. So, you got any new events coming up or anything?"

I perked up and replied, "Well other than the showcase that's it."

"Oh, yeah. When is the audition, Roxy?"

"It's next Monday at nine in the damn morning. After the audition, I'll head over to work."

Working thirteen hours a week with a cool boss had its perks. Just need better pay is all.

"Oh, aight, Ms. Roxanne. I'll remember that."

We spoke about our favorite musicians and instruments until I had to rush back to work. When I arrived back to my cubicle, I received a text from Johnson stating that he'll be picking me up at 5pm to discuss a few things.

∞

I dragged my feet to the office door and looked at the hinges, counting the little dust particles that wrapped themselves around the gold hinge. Lowering my head towards the last hinge, I noted it was bronze, old, and definitely looked like it need to be replaced. I shuddered from a consistently annoying thud at the glass.

Shelly.

I watched her lips through the small glass on the door.

"Girl, what you doing looking like that stereotypical creepy woman from those scary movies? You alright?"

I nodded and opened the door. She talked to me about her lunch and her new man. I pretended to listen as my eyes looked forward.

When we reached the library exit, she pinched my shoulder and said, "Alright, lady in the clouds. I'll see you tomorrow."

I smiled at her and wrapped one arm around her shoulders.

I watched her push the revolving door and sashayed outside. She waved at Johnson and continued on.

He really came. I wasn't really in the mood for his shenanigans. I took a deep breath, held it for a few moments and then exhaled. I watched patrons slide in and out of the revolving door until he spotted me. He waved vigorously and tapped his watch. I marched outside and stopped a few inches in front of him.

"What now, Johnson?"

"The fuck you mean what? You cancelled on me."

He raised his arms up, waiting for a hug. I walked past him and didn't stop. He rushed behind and I replied, "I e-mailed you a lot of songs awhile back and you never listened to them, Johnson."

"Yeah, so? I was busy. You singing one of your own songs? I told you they were all subpar anyway."

I shrugged as I marched over to the bus stop and plopped on the bench. I watched the sighing trees wave with the early evening wind. I heard my music playing from Johnson's phone as he sat next to me.

"Turn that down, Johnson. You don't have to be obnoxious about it."

He didn't utter a word. He listened. I slid further away from him. I hate when people blast their music in public. It's annoying. He knows that. Thankfully, the bus was arriving.

"Johnson the bus is here. Turn that down. It's making me uncomfortable."

He didn't turn it down.

"The music is good, but your lyrics and voice are subpar. We need to talk about this. I can help you. Remember, I am an artist as well."

I looked into his eyes and smiled. The bus pulled up and I retrieved my bus pass.

"Well, Johnson, I like it, Silk likes it and a few others too. More importantly, I am happy with it."

I stepped on the bus, looked back at Johnson who looked as if I told him that I shit in his mother's shoe and watched the bus door close. I remember when his fake constructive criticism made me feel lower than an anchor with a limitless chain. No more. *I'm just as talented as he is.*

Circus At Coney Island

Two drops of sweat slid down my belly as I rushed onto the stage of the Kila-Sokal theatre. I looked down at the two stains painted on my yellow dress and squinted at the bright lights above. One woman with a microphone sat in the middle of the front row and smiled at me.

She nodded and sputtered into the mic, "Okay, Ms. Patterson. You have up to five minutes to sing us a song or two. It has to be an original piece or a piece that we suggested in the e-mail. If you go over the five-minute mark, you are automatically disqualified. After you are done, you can leave the stage, go to the receptionist desk and wait for your name to be called. Payment is $200 per show and it's three shows. Is everything clear?"

I nodded.

"Good. You can begin, Ms. Patterson."

I walked over to the piano and adjusted the microphone that stood beside the stool. I heard my heartbeat as I sat and placed my hands on the keys. My ears were hot, and I could feel more beads of sweat roll down my chest. I thought about the curve in Silk's lips when she smiled. Everything within me settled.

I took a deep breath and began to play my song about loving who I am even on the days I feel low. I made sure to practice my song at least three times a day up until this moment. My heart fluttered at the parts I loved the most. When I finished, I walked to the front of the stage. I clasped my hands together, bowed and mouthed thank you to the woman. I hurried off the stage, grabbed my bag from the back of the auditorium chairs and pushed open the big red doors to the make-shift front desk. I could finally breathe normally. There was a wooden bench that already had three people sitting on it. I sat next to them and waited. I smiled and said hello to the gentleman I sat next to, but he looked ahead. *Whatever.* I hunted inside my bag for my phone. I saw two text notifications from Silk.

Hey Roxanne.
I just wanted to wish you good luck. You're going to do great. Remember: You are already talented, and you were made to sing and encourage people.

It was so quiet; I heard my cheeks rub against my jaw as I grinned at my phone. I was just about to text Annlea and Maggie when my phone rang. It was Maggie.

"Heyyy, Roxxxy," she sang into the phone.

"How'd it go? You sang the "Be You" song? You wore the red or the yellow dress?" she asked.

Before I could respond Annlea spoke up, "Roxy, where you at now? Do you get a spot?" Good ol' three-way.

The man beside me stood up and walked over to the front desk. I observed his smile evolving into a scowl as the woman at the front desk spoke to him with the phone to her ear.

"I'm still at the theatre. I'm waiting at the front desk for my name to be called. I wore the yellow dress and yes, I sang that song. I was so nervous, but it was still fun."

The guy kicked the bottom of the make-shift desk, spat on the floor and walked out of the theatre.

"Listen, I think my name will be called soon. I'll call you guys later."

They both told me okay, and I hung up. There were two ladies still seated and both of their knees were bouncing.

"Chanel Boof," the woman at the receptionist desk called with the phone in her hand.

Both of the ladies walked to the desk holding hands.

The woman spoke softly, but I was able to hear, "You didn't get a spot; however, we can put you on the stand-by list if anyone is sick or doesn't show up to the first rehearsal."

Chanel shook her head, and they both walked away. The other woman rubbed Chanel's back and whispered in her ear as they pushed open the main entrance door.

This showcase was probably full and doesn't want to make us feel as though we wasted our time. *I shouldn't have come. What a freaking waste.* I texted Annlea and Maggie that I probably didn't get it. Maggie told me to not assume anything. Easier said than done.

Twenty minutes went by and no one came out of the auditorium.

The woman who sat in the front row finally came out and looked at me, "Congratulations, Ms. Patterson. You got the last spot. Sorry for the delay, but we had a little accident with the stage light. I'll e-mail you the details, but just to summarize it here."

I observed her lips. I couldn't hear anything else. My heart was dancing, my cheeks were hot, and my arms spoke for me as I wrapped them around her.

"Thank you!"

She nodded and gently tugged me off of her. I backed up, shook her hand and walked out. The sun felt warm on my forearms and I breathed in the outside air. I got a spot. That's $600 dollars in three days just to sing my own song. As I walked over to the train station, I texted Silk to let her know I got a slot in the showcase.

I called my supervisor to let her know the good news, and she told me to just take the day off and celebrate.

Silk was calling on the other line, so I called Silk back right after I got off the phone with my supervisor.

"Congratulations, Ms. Roxanne. We gotta celebrate. Maybe after work we can go to Coney Island?"

"My supervisor told me to take the day off to celebrate. Maybe we can meet up earlier?"

"For you? Of course, Roxanne. I just got out of the shower. I'll get dressed and we'll meet by Nathanies Frankies at 2pm. How's that sound for you?"

"I'm down, Silk."

We hung up and it was 12pm. I had enough time to race home, jump in the shower, change my clothes, and meet Silk at 2pm.

∞

It took me only a few seconds before I spotted Silk across the street in front of Nathanies Frankies. Head lowered in a book, she leaned onto the packed store entrance wall with dark baggy jeans. She wore a fitted orange sleeveless top that complimented her frame. Whew, she was fine. I walked up to her and hugged her. We both uttered greetings at the same time and looked into each other's eyes. She congratulated me as we walked over to the ticket booth.

"You about to take me on some rides, Silk?"

She flashed her smile and nodded. "Damn straight I am. We gotta celebrate, Roxanne. You gettin' paid to pursue your dreams, and you did it by singing your own songs. We about to ride this Ferris wheel so we can match what's probably going on within you. How are you feeling, Roxanne?"

I could've melted right there. The sun hit her complexion just right and her scent of frankincense and myrrh was alluring.

"I feel like I'm sitting on a nimbostratus cloud."

"Ferris Wheel it is," she replied.

We spoke about our day and about the book she was reading. She loved books and adored how writers painted pictures in her head like a film. With our admission wristbands snug to our wrists, we walked straight to the Ferris wheel and waited in the short line to go high up in the sky. The lights of the nearby rides bounced around in Silk's eyes, and her muscular arms glistened from what smelled like baby oil and musk. My eyes traveled to the rising and falling of her breasts. She dipped her head to block my view of her luscious bosoms and revealed her teeth.

"Roxy? Hello." She waved.

"Oh, sorry. I was looking at your top. The color compliments your complexion."

Silk began to cackle. "Ms. Roxy, you are truly a bad liar."

"Indeed," I replied.

"Anyway, what were you saying?" I asked feeling the red rush up to my cheeks.

"So, tell me what song you sang at the audition. When is the show and how can I get tickets to support you, Shawty?"

Before I could dive into a reply, we had to show our tags and walk four steel stairs to reach the Ferris wheel. All I needed was four steps to watch her glutes stretch as she walked up the steps. Her derriere round enough to sleep on, I wondered what it looked like after a shower.

A burly man with three gold teeth and a bald head guided us to our ride car. Silk stepped aside and ushered me to slide in first. When she noticed I was secure and settled, she slid in. Sitting across from me, she leaned her head gently into the palm of her hand while her elbow occupied the table between us.

"So, how was the audition? Talk to me, Shawty."

Looking into my eyes, I stared back.

"I was so damn nervous, Silk. But once I saw the piano on the stage, I felt better. There was only one judge, and she seemed so short and cold. I thought for sure I wasn't going to get a spot."

She was all ears and engaged. Nodding and mmhming as I spilled the details. When I told her about the suspense at the receptionist desk, her eyebrows were raised, and her eyes were wide.

"Thanks for wishing me good luck."

"Of course, I support you. You're a wonderful singer and person. Why wouldn't I?"

I smiled and looked out the Ferris Wheel window.

I placed both my hands on the table and exhaled. We exchanged glances and smiles as the Ferris wheel went around. It wasn't awkward. It felt like a blanket of comfort as we enjoyed each other's silence.

Silk eventually spoke up, "So, Ms. Roxanne, what do you want out of life?"

"Oh great. Here come the interview questions. What job am I applying for tonight?"

We both laughed.

"Nah, but anyway, I want happiness, peace and a love that is solid, real, and honest. I want to sing for a living and inspire my listeners. I want to be at peace with my choices...including the choices that have caused me heavy consequences. I want to feel like sparks of thunder are cluttering my insides after I finish creating every song I write. I want to live with no regrets and to whisper my secrets to my partner at night. I want to travel and laugh with my partner. I want a partner I can create with, and we can evolve as people together. I want prosperity so I can share it with my loved ones. And no matter what I'm going through in life, I want to be able to summon joy from the pit of my belly. Because with joy, strength will follow. And vice versa. Not happiness. But joy. I want laughter even during the painful times in life."

Silk was silent. She simply beamed.

I preferred to look into people's eyes when I am conversing with them. After a while, I lose my gaze because it feels creepy. Not this moment. I let myself be lured in. I sunk deep into her eyes as she chewed on what I said and reflected before she responded. I felt stories from her eyes. I felt safe in her eyes. It felt as though a layer of silk coated around my shoulders as I looked into her eyes. As usual, everything within me settled.

"What do you want out of life, Silk?"

"I want a plethora of films under my belt, a few galleries I own, and peace. I want to move smart, not hard. I want to learn my life lessons quickly and fall in love over and over again with the same person. I want to create with my partner and evolve with my partner as well. I want to experience various cultures and countries. I want to travel and simply be. I..."

She looked out and watched the other rides. She breathed out a quiet chuckle as she heard little children screaming from one of the kiddie rides. My heart was racing trying to catch up with what was happening. *If I could just hear her say it. I'll take the risk. I'll leap.*

"I want good things, Roxanne. I want a connection that is so strong yet simplistically fits."

As we were descending, I felt my shoulders quickly rise and fall as I waited for her to say it. It was there. I knew it was. I felt it in my stomach. I refused to initiate it. She's gotta do it. I wanted to wrap my arms around her, but I knew better. The burly man tilted the ride car a smidgen as he opened the door.

"You two had fun?" he asked.

We nodded.

As I was about to scoot out, Silk wrapped her fingertips around my hand and squeezed. She took a deep breath and feathered her thumb over my hand.

"I want someone like you."

I pulled my hand back and slipped out of the car. I rushed down the steps and sped walked towards the boardwalk. The wind whizzed through my scalp as I gulped down the scene. The passing of people, lights, scents of flour and hot grease. I looked back hoping Silk was nowhere in sight. She wasn't. My phone was vibrating in my bookbag, and I let it buzz. My underarms began to tingle as I sped up the pace. I swallowed more scenery of kiddie rides and my mother's voice booming in my head:

"You too young to understand, but know that how you feel about that girl is wrong. You know it's wrong. I showed it to you in the bible many times. Stop this madness."

My throat felt as though sand was engulfing it. The balls of my feet began to ache, but I was almost there. I saw the hill that revealed the trail of wooden slabs. A clown sitting above a pool of water pointed at me and stuck out his tongue. I kept walking. I didn't belong in the circus. I slowed down once I reached the hill. I took off my shoes and shoved them in my bookbag. My phone buzzed again. I couldn't answer it. I had to leave the circus. The sand in my throat was rising. It was touching my vocals.

I finally reached the boardwalk. The beach air made the beads of sweat dripping from my skin disappear as I passed by various stores. I wanted to turn around and return to Silk, but I knew better. I walked over to a bench and crashed my buttocks onto the wooden curves. I closed my eyes and just breathed. After a few moments, I went into my bag and retrieved my phone. I held my breath as I dialed and listened to the phone ring.

"Hello?"

I finally exhaled and replied, "Hi, Johnson."

"What's up, My Queen?"

"Why did you put your hands on me?" I asked.

The sand began to dissipate.

"There you go digging into the past again. I told you. Why?"

"Yes, but I told you from the beginning I'm not the mousy type. I will always speak my mind."

"Yes, Roxy. But that was the past. I'm different."

Before I could verbally tear into him, bubbles kissed my cheeks and I turned around to see a little brown girl giggling. She smiled and waved at me. I bowed in her direction and smiled back. As her mother yanked her arm to her hips, the agitation bubbling in my chest, settled and cooled.

"You make it easy to run into another woman's arms, Roxy."

This son of a bitch.

The agitation began to bubble and boil in my chest again. My stomach was ringing bells and whistles.

"Go get her then, Johnson."

He kissed his teeth and asked, "You sure? Because I'm honestly tired of your shit, Roxy."

What a great time to dump a clown. There's sand, bubbles, a good woman, children laughing and self-respect whispering in my ear.

"I'm sure," I replied.

I ended the call and noticed the voicemail notification.

Silk. It had to be. I left her abruptly. I did a quick scan of the boardwalk and listened to her voicemail.

"Hey, Roxanne. Listen, I apologize for being so forward. I had no intentions to make you uncomfortable. I thought that you and I were on the same page as far as feelings are concerned. From now on, we'll keep it—"

I hung up.

I rapidly dialed Silk's number and closed my eyes. I let the beach, footsteps on the boardwalk and chatty humans soothe me as I listened to the ringing.

"Uh, hey, Roxy."

"Hey. I got your voicemail. Can we meet up?"

"Sure, Roxanne. Listen, I really am sorry. I shouldn't have—"

"—Silk, wait. I want good things too. I want a connection that is so strong yet, simplistically fits, too. We don't really know each other like that. But I'd like us to get to know each other. I think it's safe to say that there is a connection here that makes sense. A connection that clicks, fits and blends well."

Silk's silence was making me feel cold until she replied, "You're right. I don't know. It's something about you Roxy that's different yet feels good."

"Can we meet up next week?"

"Hell yeah."

"Cool. We'll figure out the details later. I'm sorry I walked off like that. I just...didn't know what to—"

"—Don't even worry about it, beautiful. I understand. Just text me when you get home, so I know you're safe. I hear the rides in the background. So, I assume you're still in Coney Island."

"Yeah, I am still here." I looked around. "You still here Silk?"

"Nah, I'm in a taxi now. You want me to come back? Just say the word."

"No, it's okay. I need some space to reflect and everything."

We spoke about music for a little bit and how Coney Island has changed until I reached the train station. When we hung up, my heart was still fluttering. I glided on the F train and three-way called, Annlea and Maggie about everything. They were relieved to find out that I broke up with Johnson.

"So, what's up with you and Silk?" Annlea asked.

"Nothing right now. I know she likes me, but I gotta sort somethings out within myself, you know?"

This is ridiculous. You're nothing but a selfish bitch and I can't wait for you to realize that you lost a good man. I'll be gone by then. I'm in a good and healthy relationship now anyway. Bye, Roxy.

I cackled so loudly after reading Johnson's text, my fellow artists looked back at me in the auditorium. I waved my right hand and apologized.

"Sorry, ya'll. Saw a funny picture on PicMyBiz. It won't happen again."

I slowly slid down in my chair as the other performers snickered. The woman who sat in the front row during my audition was named Ms. Castro. She gave us a brief breakdown as to what is expected of us and how we'll get paid. We had rehearsal twice a week for the next two weeks and if we were thirty minutes late, we'll be pulled from the showcase. Rehearsal was at 7pm, so I was fine. I could just stroll in right after dinner.

I blocked Johnson's number from my phone before sliding it into my back pocket. As I sat up and leaned forward, I caught a familiar face staring at me. It was

Deena, the envious troublemaker from the musical. She got up and plopped right next to me as Ms. Castro was wrapping up.

"How'd you get here? Who you know?" Deena whispered.

"I auditioned. Who did you fuck?" I asked. I was rooting for my lips to be pleasant. Guess not.

Before she could respond, we both flinched to Ms. Castro's clap.

"Alright ladies and gentlemen, let's get started with these sets. There are twelve of you. I will say your name and tell you what time you will be performing and the place you're in on the list. Got it?"

We all nodded.

I was set to perform at 8:10pm, and I was the tenth person. Deena was first and set to perform at 7:00 pm.

When Deena got up to perform, my intuition felt as though it was ringing. What was she up to? I wonder why I hadn't bumped into her during the auditions. I eventually sat a little bit closer to the stage and conversed with two of the other performers about our love for singing and making songs. We all were working at jobs we couldn't care less about while hoping to sing for a living one day.

Deena did a tap dance routine and curtsied at the end. She smiled at us as we applauded until her eyes reached my face. Her grin dropped, and she walked off the stage. Whatever. When it was my turn to perform, I sang my song about being true to yourself. Everyone applauded except for Deena. Arms folded and her eyes rolling, she sized me up from her seat.

I was relieved when I returned to my seat. Once this rehearsal was over, I was going to meet Silk at the Happy Days Diner. I made sure to tuck my purple dress into my bag, just in case I was to get messy during rehearsal. Once the twelfth performer was setting up her cello, I snuck to the back and slipped into the bathroom. I walked to the biggest stall towards the back and changed into my purple dress. It shaped my little hips well. Slowly, I switched my hips to the sink and turned on one of the faucets. I pulled out a small washcloth from my bag and lightly washed under my arms. I snagged some hand paper towels to dry and applied deodorant . As I rinsed off the cloth, I looked at my reflection in the mirror. I was still small, but the dark circles around my eyes were lighter. I imagined how I would greet Silk and what we would say. I dug into my bag and searched for my pouch that had vaginal wipes. I jolted at the bathroom door smacking the wall.

"I ain't fuck nobody to get here. I've always been a part of this showcase. For the last four years, Roxanne Patterson," Deena's voice boomed.

Refusing to look up, I rang out the washcloth, threw it away and zipped up my bag. I took a deep breath, applied on some lip gloss and flashed Deena a smile.

"Okay." I shrugged and walked right past her. "See you next week," I called behind me.

There was no way I was going to allow Deena to piss on my parade with her unwarranted misery. Yes, I didn't have to ask her who she fucked, but she shouldn't have asked how I'd gotten here.

I waved goodbye to everyone and exchanged numbers with the two performers I was sitting with. I sashayed out of the auditorium and exited the theatre. The night sky and cool breeze made me feel uplifted. I texted Silk that I was on my way to the diner. She was also on her way. The closer I walked to the bus stop, the more my stomach felt as though it was rumbling. I wasn't too sure if it was from hunger or nervousness. Either way, I needed it to settle.

∞

I arrived at the diner before Silk. I only waited for a few minutes before I saw her walking up the block. Her dark brown skin was glowing and once she saw me and revealed her pearly whites, I wanted to leap in her arms.

She softly slid her arms around my waist and whispered, "What up, Shawty?"

My arms wrapped around her as I let my body melt into hers. She smelled of her usual fragrance. I lightly mushed my cheek to hers so I could feel her face against mine.

She returned the push and said, "Yeah, I think your cheeks are soft too." She winked with her smile still plastered on her face.

We walked into the diner, picked a seat, and Silk waved her hand to one of the servers.

"So how was the first rehearsal?"

"Eh. It was fine. I met two other singers there that love to write their own music, too. Guess who else was there?"

Silk's eyes grew as she replied, "Elmo and crew ready to give y'all a decent show?"

We both giggled.

"Nah. Remember that bitter and envious chick named Deena?"

"Pfft. Oh, I thought you were going to mention someone of relevance. Oh okay. Well anyway, do you know what time you will perform?"

"Yep, I'm the tenth person and I'm supposed to be on stage at 8:10."

She nodded.

Our server finally walked up to our table, handed us menus, and placed two glasses of water on the table.

We told each other what we would order when the server returned to us. Awkward silence umbrellaed our table as I thought of how to tell her what my heart wanted to say.

I placed one hand on the table and the other on my jittering thigh.

"You good, Roxy?"

"Yeah, just excited."

"'Cause of the showcase in two weeks? I don't blame you. I knew you were going to get a spot and show your greatness. I'm excited for you too. What are you going to wear? I know you already got that song about-"

I slid my hand closer to her side of the table and interrupted

"I'm excited because I'm here with you." I sighed in relief. "There, I said it."

She looked into my eyes and leaned in. "It's a pleasure to be here with you. To be honest, I was a little nervous because of what happened in Coney Island. Once again, I'm sorry. I just thought that you maybe had some feelings for me."

She waited for me to respond, but my tongue wouldn't move. She looked down and then took a sip of her water. She placed her hand on the table and looked around at the other patrons.

I pressed my hand on top of hers and gripped lightly.

"I'm excited because I'm here with you," I breathed. I swallowed, then continued, "And because...I'm...I'm attracted to you. I have feelings for you...and if you don't have feelings for me, well, I guess I'll just have to live with that. Nothing wrong with friendship." I chuckled.

Silk smiled at me. "No, nothing wrong with friendship...but ain't nothing wrong with love, either."

My heart skipped a beat. "So...does this mean...that we're on?"

Silk licked her lips then reached over and stroked my arm. "On." she confirmed.

"I like you, Silk. It's just that, I was in a relationship and I didn't wanna send the wrong message."

"Yeah, that loser. That's why I was a bit standoffish because I ain't know what your story was, Shawty. I had my heart balled up and thrown in the trash. After that it was burned by the same person because I chose to have self-respect. You still with him?"

Her eyebrow raised; I watched her jawline clench. Phew, she had her guards up quick. I don't blame her.

"Nah, I got rid of Johnson, for good. It's a long story, but something just clicked. I deserved better, and no matter how hard I try to shove it down and denounce it...I like what I like and I want what I want."

Her face softened, and she cocked her head to the side. "What do you mean?"

"Ever since I was six years old, I saw myself growing old with a woman. But the way I was raised–loving women the way you and I do is sinful. When I was Christian, I read the verses to myself about homosexuality. So, I asked, pleaded, and fasted for deliverance. Deliverance never came. Trust me, Silk, my ass was patiently waitin' for God to snatch what I felt in my heart to be true. Even after I de-converted from Christianity, I was still homophobic towards myself. Meanwhile, I was still dating women here and there, but Mama ain't know. Johnson was supposed to be my hope. Excluding the things, he's done to me, I was hoping something in me would just fix. That I would be cured of loving women, marry a man and live happily ever after."

I checked Silk's facial expression. She was interested.

I continued, "I was never fixed because my sexuality doesn't need to be fixed. Took me awhile to realize, it's society, not me."

She smiled and placed her free hand on top of my hand.

"Thank you so much for being vulnerable with me, Roxy. I am a Christian myself. I don't believe that God would literally make me a lesbian and then turn around and call it sin. I guess I know a different version of the Christian God. I am so sorry you grew up like that. I don't know the scriptures you're referring too but—"

"—Romans 1:18 – 32, 1 Corinthians 6:9 – 10 and 1 Timothy 1:8 – 10. Some of those scriptures list other sins like murder. It's crazy...murder and authentically loving the same sex in the same group."

I had a flashback of when I was in church and praying at the altar after morning service to be delivered from wanting to be with women.

I shook my head and awaited her reply.

"Wow. Well, I am not one to act like I know it all. But I do know that I am who I am, and God loves me just the way I am." She squeezed my hand and smiled with her beautiful brown eyes.

"I feel you on that." She was a Christian who didn't care much for the Bible. I grew up in a fundamentalist home. Scripturally based and devout. I'm sure my loved ones who were Christians would surely call her lukewarm. I respected her relationship with the God she served. It's honest. She spoke about her beliefs so free and airy yet also grounded.

Our server returned to take our orders and retrieved the menus from us. As we waited for our food to arrive, we laughed at our favorite jokes from our top-five comedians. I felt as though a boulder rolled off of my shoulders and I was now floating on a magic carpet.

After we finished eating, we walked over to the promenade and sat on one of the benches. As we watched the city lights across the river, comfort blanketed over my body and I let my head fall on Silk's shoulder. She wrapped her arm around me, and I was able to rest my head on her breast. I thought of all the ways my tongue could circle, flick, and press down on her nipples.

I shot my head up and said, "Hey, why don't we get some ice cream?"

She looked at me as though I had nine heads. "Where would we get ice cream at this hour?"

"Pfft, nothing fancy. Just some ice cream from the bodega."

She shrugged and replied, "Aight, I'm down."

However, we passed the bodega, hopped into a taxi, and headed over to her place.

Leather Couches And Hot Tea

Silk had a loft in upper Harlem, and hot damn—her pad was huge! The building looked like a run-down apartment from the late 1970s. When we walked inside, it reeked of pretentious creatives and artwork that a child could create but cost millions. I was reminded that Silk was a successful documentarian. The lobby had a high ceiling and walls that were speckled with abstract paintings. There were two fat guys sitting behind a marble front desk. Silk waved at them and made small talk while I texted my friends that I was at Silk's house.

"Aight, ya'll be good," Annlea replied

She dapped them both, and I nodded at the duo. As we walked over to the elevator, she reached her hand back and wiggled her fingers. I sped up a bit, slid my fingers in between hers and walked by her side. It felt right.

"You look good in purple, Roxanne," she whispered into my ear.

The way my name slithered off her tongue made my torso warm. I looked down and saw my hard nipples and a Cheshire grin grow on her face from my peripheral.

"Thanks, Silk." I blushed.

She squeezed my hand twice, and I gazed into her eyes.

"So, you gonna invite me to this showcase or do I gotta stay home and only hear about your performance?"

As we glided onto the elevator, I kissed her hand and replied, "You know damn well you're invited, Silk."

She stroked my cheek, and I almost become silly putty on the carpeted elevator floor.

"Aight, I'm just makin' sure, Shawty."

She flashed me a smile and took a deep breath as she guided us out of the elevator. My eyes scanned her body as she walked. She wore jeans that were a tad-bit fitted, and that ass was juicy. I hoped to see it jiggle and sway from side to side soon. There were only three doors on the seventh floor, and Silk's pad was right in front of the elevator. As we walked into her apartment, we spoke about our my mothers and how we were raised. She fumbled in the dark, picking up things here and there. I stood by the door and observed the silhouettes of furniture from the moonlight that lit up her living room and kitchen. She had a high ceiling and winding staircase.

I couldn't help but chuckle to myself as I watched her bend, skip, throw things away, stop and repeat.

"So, about these lights, Silk. I hope you have them."

By this time, she was slipping off her jeans and throwing them on what looked like her couch.

"Oh. Sorry about that," she replied as she walked to me.

With each step she took, I took a step backward. Her curves were defined. She was thicker than a Wendy's milkshake during the winter and had the nerve to be tone. My hands felt hot, and my body urged to be next to her. Once my back hit the wall, I could feel her breath on my forehead. My face was damn near in between her breast. As I was about to grip her hips and slid my hands up her top, the light appeared. I looked to my left and noticed the light switch by the door. She was wearing an orange tank top and red boxer briefs.

"Oh. I didn't even see the switch there," I nervously responded.

She slid her hand up the wall and placed her other hand under my chin. *Please kiss me. Please.*

She raised my head and whispered, "Your mother will come around. But the longer you hide this, the worse the outcome will be, beautiful. Can I offer you a drink?"

I completely forgot we were talking about our upbringing and my mother. Her scent, her curves, her voice, and her eyes were enticing.

"Whatever taste you diggin' right now, Silk" I purred.

She backed up slowly and smiled. "Barrenwort tea it is, Roxy."

I placed my bag on one of the hooks she had by the door and took my shoes off.

Her spot was spacious and peaceful. I smelled Palo Santo and lavender radiating from the living room. I walked over to one out of the three couches she had and stroked the top of it. Black suede couches and a bamboo coffee table that sat in the middle of the three couches. I plopped on the couch and sat in a lotus position as I watched her make us two cups of tea. She had black marble countertops with steel appliances. She pulled out two porcelain teacups and a metal box that hoarded a plethora of teas.

"You want honey or sugar in your tea?"

I watched her lips curl into a smile as she awaited my response.

"I like honey in my tea, but I want you to come sit here next to me soon," I replied.

"Aight, aight." She chuckled.

"Let me just put this kettle on, and I'm all yours."

"Are you all mine?"

"For this moment I am. Maybe with time we can be around each other often... If that's what you're asking."

My face felt hot as I lowered my head and twiddled my thumbs.

"Why you got these black suede couches? What if you spill something on it?"

"Well, I have a special cleaner for food stains and sticky stuff. It's only one thing that I could never get out."

"What's that, Silk?"

"A woman climaxing."

"So, cum. Cum stains are hard to get out. Got it."

She burst out into laughter as she slapped her countertop.

She struggled to respond for few moments as every word she tried to let out was drowned in more laughter. Watching her laugh made me laugh.

"Damn, Roxy. For a fellow creative, I'm surprised how quick you brought that down to earth."

She walked over to the couch and sat right next to me. I shrugged and sang, "I'm just keepin' it real, Suga."

She chuckled for a few more moments.

"Hopefully, I stain it someday."

There goes that Cheshire grin again. She wrapped an arm around me and pulled me into her.

"I wouldn't mind that at all, Ms. Roxanne Patterson."

Fuck it. I want her.

As soon as she plopped next to me on the couch, I leaned into her and slowly pressed my lips to hers. She met me in the middle and my chest fluttered. I needed more. She gave me more. Nibbling on my bottom lip, I'd one up her sucking on her bottom lip and swinging my right leg over her. Straddling her soft, firm thighs, my heart raced as she cupped my bottom. I needed more. She gripped my hips and held me tighter. Our tongues played tag as our lips locked.

Something was hissing. She whispered, "Shit," when my hands dipped underneath her orange shirt. She felt like cocoa butter and satin. I let my thumbs rise up in circles until I reached her nipples. Hard and ready to be devoured, I pulled her top over her head to get a more pleasant view. She got up, with me still in the palms of her hands, and gently placed me on one of the arms of the couch. She slipped my dress up to reveal my red panties.

I needed more. She lifted my head up and lifted up my legs.

"What's next, Ms. Roxy?"

"Take over," I crooned.

The kettle whistled. She ran over to the kitchen to turn off the kettle as I stood frozen with my dress halfway up. She sped back to me and pressed her soft lips to mine. Lip locking her strawberry flavored lips felt like everything was the way it was supposed to be. She lifted my legs up once more, and I wrapped them around her thighs as I slid my hands up her shirt. I raised up my elbows, slipping her shirt above and off her head. Her nipples saluted me through her red sports bra as she flashed me a soft grin. She lifted my dress above my head and threw it nicely on her couch. She kissed me each time she unhooked one link from my bra. I draped my arms over her shoulders as she glided the straps down my arms. She dropped the bra on top of the dress and placed her hand on my heart, tracing a line from the center of my chest to the bottom of my navel.

My heart was beating faster, and I watched her mouth show me those pearly whites as she felt my heart race. Her finger reached the heart of my femininity and my legs gave her an abundant amount of space to enter. Smirking, she paused and let her tongue slither down my neck as her hands held my waist. I needed more. I tugged at her pants and struggled to unbuckle her belt. She giggled as she gently held my hands on my thighs. Her tongue swayed further down to my nipples. I closed my eyes and lifted my head to the ceiling. She let go of one of my hands and massaged my right thigh as her tongue slid passed my belly button. I massaged the nape of her neck until she got up and walked past me.

"Be right back, Ms. Roxy."

I heard her washing her hands in the back, and I guess freshening up. Sitting on a couch leg, naked and awkward, I got up and waltzed over to the kitchen as I caught my breath from what transpired. I poured hot water into two teacups for us. With my back facing the couch, I looked through the cabinets for honey or sugar. Nothing. I felt her arm wrap around my breasts and hips.

"I'm back, beautiful," she whispered into my ear as she squeezed tighter.

I raised my arms behind me to reach her neck. Her hand caressed my pelvis as the other hand cupped one of my breasts. I felt my yoni dripping at this point, so I turned around to kiss her lips. Instead, I was met with a firm grip on my ass and being lifted onto the counter tops. Making light circles over my clit, she tasted the moisture under my breast and nibbled a bit. Heavy breaths and racing hearts was the tune that played as she bent down and kissed my inner thighs.

"Fuck," I muttered.

She chuckled. Spreading my legs a bit wider, I felt her wet tongue clean up the spill that surrounded my inner lips and vulva. The more she went to work down there, the more I lost control. Gripping her hair, her shoulders, and her forearms, I needed more.

My moans were her confirmation she was doing the damn thing. Just as I was about to climax, I let my hands slide inside her bra as I massaged her breast. My body felt as though it was sitting under a sun and my legs began to shake. She stopped, lifted her head, and licked her lips.

"You taste hella good, Roxanne," she purred.

I was about to get up due to her foolishness of stopping before my first orgasm until she pinned me back and slid her two fingers inside my pussy, and that's when I lost it. I was clawing at her back, trying everything within me not to scream in pleasure, but then she moved around, and I was all in. I pushed back whatever she gave in, matching her thrusts as I called her name, her grunts making me grip her back tighter. Exploding into her hand, I wrapped my entire body around her. She carried me to the kitchen sink, washed her hands and then carried me to the couch. Placing me on her lap, she put her head back to catch her breath. Once I felt my legs again, I unbuckled her belt and slid her pants to the ground.

My turn.

The Star Reads Her Lines

Twenty minutes before it was my time to hit the stage for the showcase, I pushed the heavy curtain to the side a little and peeked at the audience. I spotted Mama, Daddy, Annlea, and Maggie sitting together. Mama's lips were pierced shut, but I knew she was excited and proud of me. Once she saw me performing, she'd be the loudest one cheering me on.

I was hoping to see Silk, but there was no sign of her. I began to tap my thigh as I rescanned the audience as best as I could, despite the blaring spotlight on the stage. I brushed the hem of my dress that stopped mid-thigh. I remember the last time wearing this; Johnson had told me that my body was too thin for it, and I didn't have the right *wow factor* to pull it off. I smiled at how the dress made me feel. I felt like a singer already in this dress, ready to love on the audience. It was a black flirty dress that was soft. Maybe cotton or nylon. Whatever the fabric was, it made me feel lovely in it.

"Don't choke out there, girl," Deena whispered behind me.

Startled by her very presence, I jolted and snapped, "Girl, don't choke on your own hate."

She backed up slowly and lifted up her hands in surrender. "Hey, hey…I was just joking. Don't get your panties in a bunch. You're about to perform soon."

"My panties are not your business. But if you must know weirdo, my panties are a bit annoyed just by your presence. Now go run along and attempt to psyche someone else out."

Before she could even respond to me, the host tapped my shoulder to let me know that I would be on in a few and should get ready. I thanked her and walked closer to the stage. Standing just behind the curtain, I watched the guy on stage play his flute.

Impressive, I must say. I was running out of breath just by watching him. I hummed my song to myself and envisioned myself on the stage, playing the piano while I sung my song. I was lured back into the present moment when I heard applause and the guy walking off the stage. I smiled and nodded at him. He looked forward and flipped his hair as he passed me. *Diva.*

I took a deep breath, counting my steps onto the stage. With each step, my grin grew, and my skin felt hotter. I guess the rehearsal light was a just a warm-up. This spotlight felt as though the theatre cut a piece of the sun and shoved it into a stage light. There were two stagehands that quickly placed a stool in front of the piano and a mic beside it. I took my seat and looked out into the audience.

There she was. Sitting in the third row, I saw her smile. I nodded in her direction, and she waved.

"Hey, everyone. You guys enjoying this showcase so far?"

I heard claps and un-synched confirmation that they were.

"Good. Now, I am may not be able to play the flute and dance like a circus performer..."

The audience chuckled.

"But I got a song I wrote, and I hope you enjoy it. My name is Roxanne Patterson, and this song is called, "Show Up for Yourself."

I took a deep breath and played with everything within me. It felt like everything was falling into place once again. My loved ones in the audience, Silk present too, and me doing what I love. Eyes closed; I sang every note as if it were my last time performing. My hands, warm as it touched the cold keys, made my heart flutter. Trusting my fingers to hit the right keys, I let my heart bleed out the words I sung.

When I finally opened my eyes and dropped my hands from the keys, I trembled from the applause and smiled at my mother's whistling. I shot up from the stool, glided to the front of the stage, beaming. I bowed, blew a kiss to Silk, and rushed off the stage.

Although the show went on, the imaginary fire in my belly sparked and cackled. I was on fire for this moment to continue. I knew for sure that singing and performing is my purpose. I high-fived a few other artists who complimented my performance. I walked over to the green room, snatched my bag from one of the hooks on the wall, and plopped on one of the beanbag chairs.

All the other performers congregated just behind the curtain, sat in the audience if they'd already performed, or were smoking just outside. I relished the solitude and moment to relive what just happened on stage. I eventually dug into my bag to retrieve my phone. A plethora of text notifications from Annlea, Maggie, and Silk congratulating me for a wonderful performance. I thanked them and shoved my phone back into my bag. I stayed in the green room until the end of the show, imagining myself singing at my first album release party.

∞

I pushed through the crowd to reach my parents in the auditorium. I hugged my father and kissed my mother. She smiled, scanned my outfit, and frowned.

"You did good, Sweetie, but that dress is way too short. Give the fellas something to imagine," she spoke.

My father shot back, "She looks fine. It isn't that short."

"Thanks, Pops."

He nodded and winked. He turned around to speak to a gentleman and pointed at me, "And here she is. My daughter."

A tall slender man in black slacks and an oversized ugly sweater nodded and reached out his hand for me to shake.

"Hey, there, Roxanne. My name is Hugh Zinglemen, and I'm from Reflection Records and I—"

My ears couldn't believe what he just said.

I burst out, "—Yes, you guys have Diane, Celie and Cookie Mins. My favorite singers!"

He softly chuckled. "Great. Well, we heard about this showcase, and we're looking for some new talent to join our roster. Can I give you my card and maybe we can have a meeting about that voice of yours?"

My mouth dropped as he handed me the card.

"Yes!" I screeched. Before he could say goodbye, he was pulled by Deena who was inquiring about the label.

"Do they have gospel singers there?" my mother asked.

"I don't know, but I know I don't want to be a gospel singer."

She rolled her eyes and tapped one of the performers to tell them how wonderful she did.

Annlea and Maggie popped up behind me with hugs, flowers, and a card. We giggled about how nervous I was and how it felt performing. Mama and Daddy made small talk with Annlea and Maggie while I eyeballed the room for Silk.

"Roxanne," my mother raised her voice. "You hear me calling you. Listen, your father and I are going to Junior's. You comin'?"

I shook my head.

"Good, more food for us. See you when you get home, baby," she said.

I kissed my father goodbye and waved at my mother.

"Hey, Ms. Roxy," Silk whispered in my ear from behind me.

I cooed as she walked around to face me.

Annlea and Maggie looked at each other and then at me.

I wrapped my arms around her and held her for a few moments. I held her tighter as she muttered *yes.*

"You did great, Ms. Roxanne. Beautiful song and spectacular delivery," she said.

She slid her hands to my waist and squeezed.

Without thinking, I replied, "My person."

"Mhmm." She beamed as she softened her grin around my waist to kiss my lips.

My heart began to race. I backed up terrified at what I just said. She pulled me back in and said,

"Don't run now. You said it already. Plus, it's mutual."

Maggie loudly cleared her throat.

I jolted backed to reality and faced Maggie and Annlea. "Besties, this is Silk. Silk, this is Annlea and Maggie."

They shook hands and made small talk while I waved goodbye to performers who passed by me.

"So, listen, we're gonna head over to Annie Ruth's Soul restaurant. Y'all two wanna join us?" Annlea asked.

Silk looked at me for answer. As much as I would like to celebrate this moment with my friends and Silk, I wanted to rush home to celebrate solo. With the card in my pocket from Hugh, I wanted to visualize myself in his office signing a contract.

"Nah. Maybe next time."

Annlea raised an eyebrow and giggled.

"Maybe we all can play some pool and get some drinks at this pool hall I know of on 31st and 10th avenue. Y'all three free next Friday?" Silk chimed in.

We all nodded, and Maggie replied, "Sounds good. Then we can get better acquainted with you, Silk. Seems like you might stick."

"I think I might stick too. We'll see." She blushed.

We all walked out of the theatre and onto the curb. I hugged Annlea and Maggie goodbye. I watched them walk to the train station up the block while Silk took a phone call. Everything was falling into place. I felt more at home with myself, my life, my dreams and with what I want.

"Hey! Earth to Roxy," Silk teased.

"Oh, what? Sorry, Silk. I was just making sure my friends arrived to the train station safely."

I finally noticed the taxi and Silk holding the yellow taxi door open.

"Oh, thanks, Silk, but I was going to take the train."

"Okay, well, now you can save your energy and nose from stink and a crowded train. Plus, you'll be next to me."

Without delay, I skipped inside the taxi and thanked Silk for holding the door open. I told the driver my address while we put on our seatbelts. Once we reached the first red light, I placed my head on Silk's shoulder. She kissed my forehead and wrapped her arm around my waist. I slipped my hand up her shirt and gently held the bottom of her breast. She leaned back and let her head rest on top of my head. My index finger began to circle around her nipple, and I desperately wished she wasn't wearing a sports bra. I began to hear her breathing as I raised my lips to her soft neck. I crept my hand up her bra and palmed her breast as I kissed her neck. Her hand disappeared up my dress as I moaned from her teasing my inner thighs. The more I separated my leg to let her in, the closer she stroked my yoni.

The taxi driver grunted lustfully and asked of us if we were alright. We both shouted yes, sat up and held each other tightly. We spoke about the showcase and how Hugh Zinglemen from Reflections Records gave me his card. She congratulated me and promised to take me out to eat to celebrate the following week.

When we arrived to my apartment, Silk offered to walk me to my apartment door. With Mama and Pops probably at Junior's, I didn't mind. She hopped out of the taxi, ran over to my side and opened the car door for me. She held out her hand to guide me out like the true gentleboi she was. We walked up the three stairs to my apartment building in silence. I opened the main entrance door and held it open for Silk. We passed by the mailboxes and walked up to my apartment door. I leaned my back against the door and pulled her close to me. She kissed me softly and slowly backed up.

"I'll see you later, gorgeous. I gotta go before this taxi man leave my ass."

We both laughed.

I leaped into her arms and squeezed her as tight as I could. She returned the clutch and kissed my cheek. We let each other go and I watched her wave as I backed up into my door again. She jogged back to the taxi and my eyes followed her until I only heard the car rolling over the gravel. I closed my eyes and took everything in. I breathed in the kiss, the taxi ride, the showcase, meeting Hugh Zinglemen and my friends.

"Thank you," I whispered.

Suddenly, the apartment door swung open, and I almost hit the floor.

"Who is she?" my mother's voice boomed above me.

I gained my balance, closed the door and looked into her eyes.

Silk is too worthy to be hidden in cupboards. I don't know what our love story will look like or if we'll even last. But I know she is too worthy to be a secret or a lie to tell my mother and a truth to my heart.

I stood up straight, held my head high and replied, "Her name is Silk."

She saw it. She knew her mental grip slowly beginning to lose its luster in my eyes.

"Have you lost your God given mind, Roxanne Patterson? And you brought her to my door for the world to see? So, you're trying to embarrass me after all I've done for you? I fed you, clothed you, taught you the ways of the Lord and this is how you repay? You really let Satan dig his claws into you, I see." Tears in her eyes, she screamed every word.

I placed my hand lightly on her shoulder to console her, but she smacked my hand away.

"Don't you touch me. Don't you dare touch me, Roxanne."

"Mama, this is who I am. I can't help it. I tried to fight it. I prayed since I was sixteen for deliverance, fasted, and tried to shut down my feelings every time a woman passed by me that I was attracted to. I can no longer give you a storyline you approve of. I can only give you my authentic self now. This is me. I loved women when I was younger, I love them just as much if not...more. "

Mama's tears vanished.

"It's repugnant. Your mouth on another woman's vagina? Disgusting. And you standing there bold and unashamed. Cocky, too. When you ought to be ashamed. It's filthy and Roxanne, God is not pleased."

The more she screamed, the more I realized how much she was trying to project.

My hands now placed behind my back, I calmly responded, "Well, I'm not ashamed. No matter how much you try to inject shame into me, it won't happen this time. You don't have power over me anymore. Mama, I love you, but this is my life. I'm not a little girl anymore."

Before I could finish, I watched her hand raise up to hit me. Once she moved her hand forward, I pushed it back, and I followed her legs buckle back a bit. She caught her balance and began to wail. Tears absent from her eyes, she wailed.

"Lord, save my disobedient child. Forgive her, Lord and please don't give her a reprobate mind. Deliver her, Lord. I've let her live with me for all these years, brought her clothes, food, games, and vacations."

I couldn't take it anymore. Prayer or not, she wasn't about to start lying to her God.

"Mama, excuse me, but I also bought my own clothes, food, vacations and you never bought me games. I don't even have a game system for that."

My mother stood in front of me in silence.

She squinted her eyes at me for a few seconds. She locked the apartment door, walked a few feet towards her door, and stopped.

"I know one thing. You either choose this home or choose to live on the streets because I will not allow no bulldagger to live in my home. Figure this mess out. You have three days to tell me what you're doing. Streets or clean sheets in this house."

"I choose freedom. I choose authenticity."

About The Author

Jasmine Farrell is from Brooklyn, NY and poetry is her first love. Internal rhyming is her favorite poetic device. She has previously published six poetry collections, *My Quintessence* (2014) Phoenixes Groomed as Genesis Doves (2016). *Long Live Phoenixes (2018)* and *The Release Series (2020)*. She is committed to using her personal experiences to inspire those on a similar path. She is currently working on the second installment of *Sloppy*.

Personal Website:
http://www.jasminefarrell.com

Social Media
Instagram: @Justbreathejasmine
Twitter: @authorjfarrell

www.ingramcontent.com/pod-product-compliance
Lightning Source LLC
Chambersburg PA
CBHW021331190726
48288CB00003B/1051